# ALSO BY ZACH FORTIER

## Non-Fiction
CurbChek
Street Creds
CurbChek Reload
The CurbChek Collection
Hero to Zero
Landed on Black

## Biography
I Am Raymond Washington

## Fiction
### The Director Series
Baroota: The Hunting Ground
Cachibaché: Book II in The Director Series
Izadi: Book III in The Director Series
Chakana: Book IV in The Director Series

## Science Fiction
### The Overseer Series
Volk: Book I of The Overseer Series

Scan the QR Code to the left to go to
Zach's page on Amazon

# CHAKANA

## BOOK FOUR OF THE DIRECTOR SERIES

## BY AWARD WINNING AUTHOR
## ZACH FORTIER

## CHAKANA
Copyright © 2018 Zach Fortier

This is a work of fiction. Names, characters, businesses, places, events and incidents are either the products of the author's imagination or used in a fictitious manner. Any resemblance to actual persons, living or dead, or actual events is purely coincidental.

Published by

Steeleshark
press

ISBN-13: 978-0692-18214-7
ISBN-10: 0-692-18214-4

Visit the author at:
Website: *www.zachfortier.com*
Goodreads: *www.goodreads.com/author/show/5164780.Zach_Fortier*
Blog: *www.authorzachfortier.blogspot.com*
Facebook: *www.facebook.com/authorzach.fortier*
Twitter: *www.twitter.com/zachfortier1*
Instagram: *http://www.imgrum.org/user/zachfortier/505378433*

*"There is no hunting like the hunting of man,
and those who have hunted armed men long enough
and liked it never care for anything else thereafter."*

~ **Ernest Hemingway** ~

# Contents

*"Death never takes the wise man by surprise,
he is always ready to go."*

**~Jean de La Fontaine~**


*"C'est double plaisir de tromper le trompeur."*
*(It is a double pleasure to deceive the deceiver).*

**~Jean de La Fontaine~**
in Book II (1668), Fable 15 (The Cock and the Fox)

The **Chakana** (or Inca Cross) is a stepped cross
made up of an equal-armed cross indicating
the cardinal points of the compass and a
superimposed square.
The meaning of the cross is unknown.


"I'm waiting
I'm hating
Realize
Start hiding"

**~Breaking Benjamin~**
Breath

# CHAPTER ONE

For two weeks, Svetlana and Buffy had been searching, compiling and trying to organize a dossier on The Director. Nick had asked that they find as much as possible to give him some kind of insight into who their enemy was. He'd hoped they would find some kind of intelligence file or personality profile on the man. He'd been in government service most of his adult life and undoubtedly had been cleared for above a Top-Secret clearance. That meant he'd had every aspect of his life, every misstep, every hiccup logged, documented and retained somewhere. They just had to find it.

The search had been difficult. To find anything meaningful or substantial had been tedious. The Director had been insanely cautious about what appeared on the Web concerning any aspect of his life, his past or any action he had taken. Anything that might be embarrassing or used as leverage against him had been scrubbed from not only the Web but every database in the government and private sector. For two weeks, they'd found nothing worth their time. They'd hacked, forced, cajoled, and muscle fucked (as The Driver referred to it when he threw the considerable power of every one of his servers behind a hack) every database on The Driver's considerable list of previously hacked sites. Scraps and minor references and details were all they found. The Director was a ghost. Svetlana had found his name during her search of The Driver's computer, but it led nowhere. The name might as well have been an alias. A one-way street that leads to a dead end, from which you couldn't return.

Then one day they hit the mother lode. It was a remarkable find. Somehow, some way Buffy was poking around the database of a highly classified top-secret government surveillance program known as STATE-ROOM. She had found nothing even remotely related to The Director and was about to leave the site before her illegal intrusion was discovered when she found a file named "Shāh Māt." When she opened it, she was elated to discover the file was dedicated entirely to one thing, one person. After two weeks of frustrating searches, the entire life history of The Director dropped into their laps. Buffy let out a victorious feral scream that gave some indication of the intense pressure they both had felt. "YES!" Svetlana jumped out of her chair, surprised at the sudden display of emotion. The find validated their abilities to replace The Driver in the team's hacking and computer skills department.

Buffy quickly copied the file as fast as she could. It took some time as the file's size was considerable, six Gigs to be exact. She assumed it must have a lot of photos and or video to be so large. It had four pictures and no videos. Six Gigs of data, and only four photos. Buffy was immediately suspicious and ran a check of the file to look for hidden files or content. Something the government had installed to track the file. She found nothing. The file was clean. Buffy and Svetlana double and triple checked the files, and when they were convinced the folder was legitimately safe to use, they copied it to a thumb drive. Finally, they relaxed, hugged, and high-fived. Svetlana did a small victory dance, literally dancing there in the new and improved Bat Cave 2. Then they left the Bat Cave to find Bexx and tell her the good news.

Nick and Bexx were walking inside the fenced-in area of the missile facility. They'd inherited it from Arthur just before he died. Nick had healed mentally from the toxic mind game he had played with The Driver, but the echoes of The Driver's claims haunted him. He was on guard now, edgy - more edgy if that was possible - than before the lethal conversation. For Bexx, the change in Nick was a constant reminder that she'd allowed, if that was the correct word, him to interrogate The Driver. She never imagined The Driver would be effectively able to penetrate Nick's mental shielding. Their conversation had changed him. When he slept, if he slept, it was a fitful sleep, filled with nightmares, dark images and nearly always ended with him coming off their bed like a pit bull in an illegal dog fight, snarling, swinging blindly, screaming threats at enemies that weren't there. Trying to kill the ghosts of his past, and enemies in his present. Nick was a mess, and it was never more obvious how broken he really was than in this early morning display of rage and fury.

Bexx felt responsible for Nick's mental slide backwards. He'd been relaxed, happy even, if the word could be applied to someone like Nick, when he thought The Director was dead. Now he felt vulnerable, the betrayal of The Driver and the implication that Bexx had betrayed him as well had opened a wound that wouldn't heal soon. Even more than that, he realized his vulnerability to The Director. If The Driver knew so well how to manipulate him, to understand and exploit his carefully guarded weaknesses, so did The Director. Nick needed a weapon to counter this, but he had none, so they walked and talked. Bexx realized after eavesdropping on a conversation between Nick and Special K that he mentally processed everything as he moved, paced, fidgeted.

She kept him moving and talking as a means to help him heal. She listened as he talked and processed, finally coming to an understanding of what his world had been and how he had survived by seeing and listening acutely. For Nick, survival had come at a price; his mind was focused on details, looking for anything that would provide a warning of betrayal, deception. When he missed what he felt in hindsight was an obvious sign of betrayal, it was crippling. There could be no mistakes. Over and over again he'd had this point driven home in his life. Be alert, be aware, never relax.

Svetlana and Buffy approached them as they walked and talked. From the way the two moved as they approached, Nick could see they were excited. Their steps were too quick, light, purposeful. Their arm swings tight and sharp, eyes locked on him and Bexx. Their strides locked in unison. Their confidence and excitement were apparent. They'd had a breakthrough in their search for information on The Director.

Bexx and Nick listened as Svetlana and Buffy explained what had happened. They found a file that was huge, loaded with details about The Director. It was an unexpected breakthrough given the difficulty they'd experienced finding anything of value about his life and experiences. When Buffy explained the random location of the file and name of the file, Nick perked up.

"Shāh Māt? You're sure that was the title of the file?"

"Yes," Buffy replied, curious that was what caught his attention. "Why?"

"Spell it for me," Nick replied.

"S-H-A-H-M-A-T," Buffy replied.

Nick smiled and replied, "Interesting." Before Buffy or Svetlana could ask the obvious question, Nick continued. "Okay, can you print it all out and bring it to me when it's done? I need paper copies. I need to touch them, hold them. Great job! Congrats to both of you!" Nick reached out and fist bumped them each, smiling. Nick stopped smiling, then turning to Bexx he said, "I think we should keep this quiet, for now, let's keep the file between us four, no one else needs to know. Agreed?"

Bexx was silent for a moment, assessing the outcome of keeping the file a secret. She turned to Svetlana and said, "Well? What do you think? Keep it quiet for now?"

Svetlana looked at the ground, thinking. Then at Nick. "I can't see a reason why it needs to be a secret. Is there something we need to know?"

Nick paused. "After The Driver came clean, I realized I don't know what else I've missed. Could be nothing, but isn't it better to be careful? We won't get many more chances."

They all agreed to keep the file a secret for now, if for no other reason than to appease Nick's anxiety.

They talked to Bexx a few minutes more and then turned to print out the huge file. After they left, Bexx turned to Nick and asked, "Shāh Māt? That means something to you, obviously. What does it mean?"

Nick smirked, "I don't know if it means anything, really. The word origin is Persian, it means Check Mate in English. But in Persian, the direct translation means 'The King is Helpless'". Nick looked at her directly. "'The King is Helpless,' think about that. Who names a file on The Director, hopefully containing every detail of his life, The King is Helpless? Interesting implications there, Bexx, very interesting."

Bexx looked at him questioningly. "You play chess?"

"I love chess. I study chess strategy. I'm not real good at it, but I love the idea of the game. Our Director has been playing chess with us the entire time, sacrificing his pawns, moving in for the kill. Remember Star

Trek chess?"

Bexx rolled her eyes. "Yes, I remember, three-dimensional chess-boards."

"You were listening!" Nick smiled again. He held up his right hand, fingers splayed apart in a V, the typical Vulcan greeting. "May the force be with you, Bexx!"

Bexx shook her head and said, "Unfortunately, yes, I was listening. Let's keep walking, funny man."

In the basement of an ancient government building less than a thousand miles from the missile facility, another man walked with that same excitement and purpose Svetlana and Buffy displayed. He reached the large metal door and pushed the buzzer. He waited; there were lights on the outside of the door, red and green, and the meaning was obvious. You're not allowed to enter until the green light glowed, and the internal lock was released with a loud click. He waited, the light was red. Click, and the light was green. He pulled the door open and entered the office.

The room was pitch black, and light classical music played from somewhere inside the office. He had never been allowed to see the entire office, so he had no idea how large it was. Or even who worked inside. No one knew. No one had ever seen anyone leave or enter the office. Whoever worked inside the office never spoke, information was left on the desk, a briefing was given, and then The Messenger was dismissed with a wave. The Messenger waited for his eyes to adjust to the darkness before taking another step. Once, he'd made the mistake of stumbling forward into the darkness and immediately stumbled and fallen over some minor piece of furniture, falling flat on his face and breaking his nose. The lesson had been painful and well learned. Wait until your eyes adjusted to the ink black darkness of the office. When there was light, it came from a computer screen, the brightness adjusted to the bare minimum.

His eyes adjusted as he waited for the hand signal to approach. He could barely see the outline of a human, a silhouette that gave no hint of the gender or age of the person he would be briefing. The lack of any information about the occupant of the office had at first been unnerving and made him uncomfortable. Eventually, he learned to appreciate the neutrality the dark provided. The lack of any eye contact and voice communication forced him to prepare briefings that were detailed and all-inclusive. Finally, the silhouette leaned back, and he saw the head raise. A signal to begin the briefing.

"You asked to be informed if the Shāh Māt file was ever accessed. It has been. A hacker group has been searching the Web for the past couple of weeks for any and all information on one of our own."

The silhouette leaned forward, arm outstretched towards The Messenger. The nonverbal meaning was clear, he reached out and handed the briefing he had prepared over. The file opened, and the silhouette motioned with a hand rotating in circles to continue.

"As you know, Shāh Māt is the file that refers to the classified background information of Robert Taylor, the Director of both the *National Intelligence Agency* and the *Defense Intelligence Agency.* Those are his publicly acknowledged offices. He is also the Director of the *National Geospatial Agency,* among others. The list is extraordinary, as you are well aware. This makes him one of the most powerful men in any of the intelligence branches."

The silhouette nodded.

"We initially thought the hacker was one of our own, hired by the NSA and under their employment for the past several years. His electronic signature is all over the hack, the computer and the tracking software is his. However, his hacking pattern has changed. As you know, we possess software that enables us to monitor the pattern a hacker develops. Every hacker has a pattern, a digital method or thought process that develops and enables us to identify them from their pattern of attack. It is 98% accurate. Although the hardware displayed by this hacker has been employed, the pattern is unique, unlike any other, he has displayed in the past. Additionally, for the past few years, he has been working specifically for Robert Taylor, the subject of the Shāh Māt files. I believe he has been compromised and someone else is using his alias, equipment, and software while maintaining his hacker identity. We have investigated his latest queries, and their software language pattern matches his, their hacking pattern does not. Am I clear? It's not him. Shall I have his equipment shut down remotely?"

The silhouette's head shook back and forth, No, and quickly removed a piece of paper from a small notepad on the desk and wrote something and then handed it across the desktop. The pen strokes were quick, and if The Messenger was honest, the silhouette suddenly seemed... excited? Agitated? He couldn't be sure.

The note read: Do we know who it is that has taken over our hacker's equipment?

"No, the footprint, if you will excuse my analogy, is unique, and never before recorded in our software. Whoever this is, they are new to us."

The silhouette leaned back and disappeared into the darkness of the high-backed La-Z-Boy office chair. The one-sided conversation was over unless The Messenger had more to add to the briefing. The Messenger turned and began to walk towards the door. Briefly, he wasn't sure, but he thought he heard a whisper, so quiet, so subdued it must have been in his imagination. He stutter-stepped for a moment, stumbled and then regained his composure. It must have been his imagination. The person behind the silhouette had never uttered a word to him in the entire fifteen years of his service. Not a single word. He left the office and walked to the elevator thinking, trying to decide if he'd heard the whisper or not. It must have been his imagination. The comment made no sense in the context of the briefing he'd given. He thought he'd heard a voice, neither distinctly male nor female, whisper in a foreign accent, "Your move."

## CHAPTER TWO

It had been four hours since Nick started taking apart the printed version of the Shāh Māt file. Bexx came into the room he had chosen to read it in and sat watching him. He never even acknowledged her. She realized after twenty-minutes of watching him, he was totally immersed. He had no idea she was there. She cleared her throat; nothing.

"Nick?" she said quietly.

Nothing. He didn't move. Finally, she got up and walked toward him and put her hand on his shoulder. Nick flinched and looked up at her, startled.

"How goes the studying?" she asked.

Nick raised his eyebrows. "It goes. Some very dark stuff here. I really don't want to verbalize it until I wrap my head around it. There's a lot here to process. Too much, really. This isn't what we thought, Bexx, something is wrong with this file. No one compiles this kind of information for a security clearance. It's far too detailed, too much depth. I can't imagine what the reason would be to go into this much depth. It's incredible the time that's been spent tracking down every single person who ever had contact with The Director. Someone, besides us, is very interested in what makes him tick. For example, every bio has a name, date of birth, relatives, schools attended. This file goes back to his childhood, like preschool, and even before that. Who does this? And why?"

Bexx listened and tried to understand what Nick was seeing, then finally spoke up and said, "Dinner is ready. JT cooked tonight, and you know what that means!"

Nick smiled. "Dude has some awesome skills as a chef! A plus we never counted on when he joined the team. Let's go eat!"

During the meal, Special K sat and watched Nick and Bexx from across the room, saying nothing but watching intently. Finally, she spoke up.

"Nick, how would you feel about joining the team for a sparring session tomorrow? We spar every day, all of us. Well, almost all of us. Even Diamond Dave spars. Everyone attends. Everyone except you. I mean, you are a member of the team, right? Care to join us?"

Bexx's eyes hardened as Special K continued on her rant until finally, Nick answered.

"Sure, I don't see why not." Nick smiled and looked at JT. "Probably could use a match or two to knock off the rust and stay sharp. What do you think, JT?"

JT looked at Bexx and then Special K. He said nothing but nodded, yes.

Nick smiled at Special K. "Plan on it. What time again?"

Special K replied to Nick but glared at Bexx, returning her gaze defiantly. "Morning workout is always at eight-thirty sharp! 'Course you'd know that if you ever attended."

The tension in the room was immediate. The team watched the exchange as Nick pretended not to be aware of the tension. Given the prior relationship between Bexx and Special K, he now understood the team's personal dynamics a bit more than he had before.

Nick smiled. "I'm guessing you're going to volunteer to be my sparring partner?" he said to Special K.

She replied with barely veiled sarcasm, "Definitely. Looking forward to it!"

JT shook his head but said nothing to the group. He approached Special K and quietly whispered, "You may want to rethink that decision," and stared directly at her, unflinching.

Special K shrugged her shoulders and continued to eat as JT shook his head and walked away.

The next morning, Special K awoke early and was first from the team in the gym. She wanted to be warmed up and ready before Nick arrived. JT arrived next and asked her directly, "Is there any way I can talk you out of this?"

She shook her head no. He continued. "Apparently, you weren't listening when I told you about Nick. Now you'll find out for yourself. Don't say I didn't warn you when it's over." He turned and walked away.

The team arrived in a group about thirty-minutes later, followed by Nick and Bexx. JT took them through their usual warmups, and then they all gathered around the sparring area. JT asked the obvious question, hoping Special K would have a sudden change of heart. "Who wants to go first today?"

Special K spoke up, "Me! I want to go first!" And then she turned to Nick and said, "Are you up to it, or have you changed your mind?"

Nick looked at her, showing no emotion. He could feel the tension rising in the room. "Sure, I'm up for it." He had no idea what Special K was up to, but obviously, she had an issue with him. What else was new? Chick had a bug up her ass about him from day one. Shit, she had mad dogged him the very first day in the van on the way back from Spokane. At least now he knew why. Spar? Sure, they could spar. Might do her some good to get it out in the open, and maybe she would finally get up out of his ass.

Nick joked, "Remember I bought you Chinese Food when no one else would? Remember that!"

Special K glared back.

The first round ended with no real winner. Special K was fast, she had fast hands and could kick with equal speed and accuracy. Nick stayed out of range and watched for an opening.

Round two was dirty and ended with both fighters exchanging significant blows. Then came the third round. Just as the round started, Special

K spit out her mouth guard and began talking trash to Nick, telling him he was too old, soft, etc..., then he landed a right uppercut that stunned her. Nick backed off and let her recover. He dropped his guard and approached her, asking if she was okay. Special K had a mouthful of blood and snot. The fight wasn't going as she had planned, and now to make matters even worse, Nick was asking if she was okay.

Special K inhaled a large breath through her nose, evacuating all the snot, mucus and blood that had accumulated there and then gathered it into her mouth and spit it in Nick's face. She managed a "Fuck you, asshole" before Nick snapped.

Nick heard the intake of air through Special K's nose, and although he halfway knew what it meant, he didn't expect her to spit the contents of her mouth at him; he thought she would spit it out of the ring. The disgusting act flipped a switch in Nick's head, and the sparring now ceased.

JT shut his eyes, and whispered, "Shit."

A fight began. A real fight.

The flurry of blows that rained down on Special K was unexpected. The team was stunned by her action and then even more so by the violence that erupted. For Bexx and JT, time slowed down as they each tried to get into the ring as quickly as possible. Bexx tried to grab Special K, while JT went to Nick. All Nick saw was an opponent.

JT tried to reason with Nick, saying, "It's me, bradah, it's me."

Nick saw nothing but an enemy, a face that belonged to an enemy he had tried to kill in the past. Nick swung and missed, and JT wrapped him up and tried to talk him down. They wrestled, and Nick growled and struggled to get free. Emotionally, he was escalating, and JT could see immediately this wouldn't work.

He yelled to Bexx, "I need you over here, you're the only one who can reach him now. I don't want to have to fight him over this stupid shit. Let me take care of her, you take care of Nick."

Meanwhile, the rest of the team sat motionless, stunned, and speechless. Diamond Dave was reminded of the incident in the kitchen and unconsciously rubbed his eye as he shook his head. No way was he getting into the ring to assist.

Bexx nodded, and JT managed to toss Nick into a corner and quickly switched places with Bexx.

Nick spun around, ready for JT to attack; in his mind, they were back on the streets, back to the day they met. They were in a battle for survival. There was no other choice but to win any way you could; to lose was not an option. JT was gone, and Bexx stood in his place.

Nick snarled and tried to get past her. She stood in his path, moving as he moved, talking calmly. "Nick, it's over, ease down, calm down, breathe." She just kept repeating the phrase over and over. Slowly, she began to reach him. It wasn't a consistent drop in rage; randomly, he would erupt again, and the process would start over. Eventually, he was breathing rapidly but not furiously.

He stopped pacing, and she asked, "Would you let me clean you off?" Nick nodded.

Bexx held up a cloth and let him see it. "Just going to wipe off the spit, okay?" He nodded, still unable to speak. He was calmer but not yet sane. She came closer, talking quieter. "Don't think you'll be able to find another sparring partner after today, what do you think?" She smiled as she wiped the bloody mass of snot off his face.

JT found Special K unconscious. In the short few moments it took to get into the ring, Nick had slammed her head into the corner post several times, knocking out several teeth and breaking her nose. He then pulled her off the post and threw her to the ground. Dropping immediately on top of her, he started driving his knee into her ribs. Then JT arrived, pulling Nick off her and most likely saving her life. The day's sparring was now over. The Mentalist jumped into the ring with her medical bag and went to work on Special K, while Bexx gently coaxed Nick from the gym. Best to get him out of the area before something else happened.

Later that night, Bexx called a meeting. It was quick and short.

"Anyone else have any issues with Nick not training with the team?" she asked.

The team was silent. No one spoke. She continued. "Now you realize what I faced back in Moses Lake when you all went to town, and I brought Nick to the team. You all came back to find the house destroyed and wondered what had happened. You now have some idea of the fight that occurred. If any of you has an issue with Nick, come to me. Let's not be stupid like this again. Any questions?" There were none. Bexx turned to The Mentalist and asked, "How is she?"

"She lost a few teeth, has a concussion and a few broken ribs. I think she'll be okay. She doesn't remember much after the second round. Probably a good thing," The Mentalist replied.

Bexx nodded. "Training will continue tomorrow; Special K is exempt for now. Are there any questions?" No one said a word. Svetlana finally raised her hand. "May I say something?"

Bexx paused for a moment. Svetlana was Special K's sister. The last thing Bexx wanted was more tension on the team. But she had asked for comments; lesson learned, now she was committed. Bexx nodded and waited to see what Svetlana would say.

"My sister has a way of getting under your skin. Don't think for a minute she didn't know what she was doing. I love her dearly, but believe me, we fought our entire childhood just as fiercely as you saw today. She hates to lose. Today she felt she was losing, and you saw the result. She needs to own this. This is on her, no one else. Don't feel sorry for her. Make her own this."

Bexx nodded, saying nothing. This wasn't what she expected Svetlana to say, but coming from her, it carried more weight than if she had spoken the exact same words. They both knew Special K intimately and knew who she was and what she was capable of. The meeting was over.

# CHAPTER THREE

The next day, the team returned immediately to normal. Svetlana's comment had provided the perspective needed to move on from the fight. Nick was left alone to study the Shāh Māt files. The next two days were spent the same way. Finally, Nick finished the first run through the file. He sat deep in thought, staring, his eyes not seeing the wall he stared at. The lack of visual input allowed him to focus. Finally, he began to pace, his hands diving deep into his pant pockets and retrieving the handful of quarters he kept there. Immediately, the action of rolling them from top to bottom began as Nick began to process the information recorded in the file.

The Director: Robert Taylor

The Director was scheduled to meet the *House Select Committee on Intelligence,* and more specifically he would be briefing the *Subcommittee on Terrorism, Human Intelligence, Analysis, and Counterintelligence* in a classified briefing afterward. The meeting was scheduled for 0900 hours; it was 0915, and The Director was just now approaching his custom Black Chevy Tahoe. It was customized for his protection and particular needs. The Director had been confined to a wheelchair since an accident in the late 1990s. His confinement to the chair and the reason for it was a very well-guarded secret. Much like *Franklin Delano Roosevelt,* The Director wanted no image of him seated in a wheelchair ever to gain national attention.

The Director was met by his driver and aide, Ian. Ian was not his real name. Upon accepting the position as The Director's driver and aide, Ian had been required to change his name. Every driver The Director had employed were required to change their names to Ian. No one ever asked why; it was part of the job. Your identity, your life, your every breath was now subordinate to The Director's every need. He made sure that point was emphasized and reinforced every time he addressed his driver. Their identity belonged to him.

Ian opened the rear door to the Black Chevy Tahoe and spoke gently but firmly to The Director. "Sir, the committee awaits your arrival."

"Yes, Ian, I'm aware. They can wait. It serves them well to understand even at their alleged lofty positions, they may still be required to wait for a true patriot."

The Director reached for Ian's right arm, signaling that it was appropriate for him to now assist in moving him from the specialized custom wheelchair to the enlarged back seat of the Tahoe. Ian knew to wait for this signal. The previous driver had after seven years of service made the critical mistake of reaching for The Director before he was ready to be assisted. A very slight faux pas to most, which cost him dearly. The implication of the premature reach to assist The Director was a lack of subordination and submission. To The Director, it displayed a complete lack of respect. That version of Ian awoke the following week in a black site prison located in an undisclosed location. He had been castrated and his tongue removed. He would never again see a friendly face or speak to anyone. The arm that had touched The Director without permission had been crushed in a hydraulic press. He was left on the floor of a filthy cement cell, without any means to manage the pain of his now useless and crushed arm. He screamed until his voice failed and only silent forced expulsions of air escaped his lungs.

When the current version of Ian was offered the job, he was made aware of the mistake of his predecessor and the resulting punishment. Still, he agreed to accept the position. This was important to The Director. He demanded complete subordination.

"Ian, announce to the committee that I'm en route as soon as we leave the parking structure. I want them to be ready to commence with the briefing when I arrive. Let them know I expect the usual amenities will be in place as well."

"Yes, sir. Will you require anything else, sir?

"No, Ian, that will be all."

"Shall I close the window, sir?"

The Director nodded silently.

Ian nodded in return and then closed the glass that separated the front area of the Tahoe from The Director's secured compartment.

The briefing was conducted behind closed doors and went well, with one exception. The newest senator from the state of Iowa interrupted The Director as he began the briefing by asking what caused the delay in his attending the briefing at the agreed upon time. The Director looked at every member of the committee to ascertain if any of them felt so inclined to challenge his position. Not one of them met his inquisitive gaze. Most looked down, and some looked away. One member covered his eyes and grimaced. At one time or another, everyone on the committee had made this mistake, but no one talked about the result of challenging The Director. No one would admit what it had cost them. The newest member of the committee would learn the hard way; seems they always had to learn the hard way.

The Director took out a piece of scratch paper and made a mark. One line on the paper. The committee knew what this meant. Beads of sweat broke out on several foreheads, and breathing increased, as did heart rates; barely controlled anxiety from reliving the painful memories would do that to a senator. More water was poured, and full glasses were brought to now trembling lips.

When the meeting was over, the newest senator on the committee had interrupted The Director seventeen times. Seventeen hash marks were on the piece of paper. The Director concluded his briefing, then folded the piece of paper and put it in his briefcase. When he was ready, Ian wheeled him from the large committee briefing room.

Senator William Stanifer was the newest member of the House *Subcommittee on Terrorism, Human Intelligence, Analysis, and Counterintelligence.* He had been elected by a landslide in his home state of Iowa. He came to Washington with a mandate to shake things up and let the powers that be know the people of Iowa were tired of being led by old men afraid to challenge the status quo. William Stanifer was sent with that message in hand. Challenge everything! He took pride in the assignment to the Subcommittee on Terrorism. Brash, arrogant, and unafraid, he walked with his head high from the meeting, feeling confident he'd made it known he would not be kowtowing to any of the Washington elite.

Stanifer, Bill to his co-workers, approached the elevators that led upwards from the basement where the briefings had been held. The elevator on the right was full, and not one of the senators attempted to hold the door to allow him on. Bill smiled; it was fine with him. Better they know now, things were about to change. He pushed the up button and waited.

Another younger senator approached and saw Bill. He stopped and tried to find a way to not be noticed: too late, Bill called out to him.

"Ron, come join me. I just called the elevator, it should be here any moment. The rest of the old guard has already taken the elevator on the right. Packed in like sardines, they were, and they made it perfectly clear I wasn't welcome." Bill laughed.

Ron tried to find a subtle way to refuse the elevator ride, but there was no other way out of the basement that didn't set off alarms. The fire exits were automatically set to go off if the doors opened to the stairways leading up. Ron was stuck. He smiled awkwardly.

The door to the left elevator opened, and Bill stepped in and held the door for Ron. "Come on, man, what're you waiting for, an engraved invitation?"

Ron got on the elevator. For a moment, he thought perhaps Bill would shut up, perhaps sharing this elevator really wasn't a big deal. He was wrong.

"So, what's the deal with the guy in the wheelchair, Director Taylor? Jesus, the guy shows up late, no apology, and no one calls him on it. To be honest, I'd no idea he was confined to the chair. Seems like a situation the press would've picked up on by now, someone should've mentioned it. I was told the guy is formidable and one of the most respected and feared men in Washington. Unless that chair turns him into *Optimus Prime,* I saw nothing to be impressed by. I mean, he'd have to have some amazing Transformer skills to pull off that reputation. Think he ever wakes up with an erection and doesn't know it? I bet he feels nothing from the waist down. That'd be a bitch, huh? I mean, what's the point of living life if you can't screw an intern now and then?" Bill laughed.

Ron broke out in a sweat. He had to make clear he didn't agree with Bill, and fast. "If you know what's good for you, you'll shut the hell up. Don't say another word. Just shut the hell up."

Bill laughed. "Why? What's old *Ironsides* going to do, run me over with the wheelchair? Transform into a *Decepticon* and rip me a new asshole? Fuck him! He was late, I was on time. He needs a reality check. Bill Stanifer is on the Hill now, and *Herbie* and his love bug wheelchair need to get to our meetings on time! I'm a senator, for Christ's sake, and I was there on time. He's just an appointed position. I was voted into office."

Ron had to salvage this quickly. He shoved Bill against the wall of the now rising elevator. "Director Taylor is one of the most respected men in Washington. It would behoove you to keep that in mind before you say anything else. Our nation owes him a considerable debt! You have no idea what a critical role he plays in keeping our people safe and our country at the pinnacle of power in today's complicated world. We all owe him our unquestioning gratitude, Senator."

Bill was smiling. "Jesus, Ron, you sound like Marv Albert riding Michael Jordan's dick in the NBA Finals. Need a breath mint, or do you leave the taste of Director Taylor's worthless shriveled cock on your breath all day long? What the hell, man? I mean, do you polish his balls in your spare time?"

The door finally opened, and Ron erupted from the elevator. Sweat pouring down his face, he was breathing heavily as he ran down the hallway.

Bill shook his head and laughed. This was why he came to Washington. Time to shake the tree, rattle a few skeletons in some of the older senators' closets. He walked confidently to his new office and nodded at his secretary. Walking to his new desk, he sat and leaned back in the plush leather chair.

Smiling, he spoke quietly, "The world is my oyster, bitches. Billy Stanifer has arrived!"

Later that night, The Director reviewed the footage and audio files from the elevator. He replayed the video file, listening to the recorded conversation over and over. Finally, he stopped and picked up the phone on his desk.

A voice on the other end answered, "Yes, sir, how may I be of service?"

"Schedule a torture date for the junior senator from Iowa. I want full video coverage. Let me know when the room and guests will be ready."

"Yes, sir," the voice continued, "do you have any specific requests for Senator Stanifer?"

"No, use your considerable imagination, leave no stone unturned. I have it on good authority the senator has a particular interest in an intern; that may be useful to you. I want this particular session to be memorable. The next time the junior senator from Iowa speaks to me, I want to clearly hear the terror in his voice."

"I'd be delighted, sir," the voice on the phone spoke calmly.

The Director hung up, smiling wickedly. The junior senator from Iowa would soon learn a painful lesson in humility and respect.

# CHAPTER FOUR

S enator Stanifer was working in his office when the phone rang. His secretary answered the call and a few moments later knocked at the door that separated their two offices.

"Senator, I have a message from Director Taylor."

"Yes? What is it?"

"He's hosting a dinner and would like you to attend. The invitation includes a guest of your choice."

The senator smiled; already his work and attitude were being recognized and rewarded. Director Taylor had recognized that he was not a man who would be bullied into falling in line behind the status quo, business as usual, I scratch your back and you scratch mine attitudes of the Washington elite.

"Shall I tell him you'll be attending, sir?"

"Yes, and I'll be bringing a guest as well. Where's the dinner?"

"Director Taylor's driver says he will have a car brought to your apartment and provide you with transportation. The car will arrive tonight at seven pm."

"Excellent. Contact Senator Bennett's office and let me know when you have him on the line."

A few minutes later, the secretary returned to the office. "I have Senator Bennett on the line, sir."

Bill smiled and picked up the phone. "Ron, you will never guess who just invited me to dinner!"

There was no remark for a minute, and then Ron asked, "Who?"

"Director Taylor! Guess the old man realized it was better to make peace with the new blood rather than fight Billy Stanifer for every scrap our committee would dole out for the next six years. I told you he'd see the light. Think I'll invite that hot little intern I mentioned to you earlier."

Ron said nothing for several minutes. "Listen, Bill, maybe you should rethink this. I mean, there is plenty of time…."

"Nonsense, what's to rethink? Director Taylor will be eating out of my hand like a tamed circus lion in no time. Just thought I would share the news, brother. You might want to attach your wagon to mine because the sky is the limit. William A. Stanifer is in Washington now, and the status quo is about to change for the better."

Ron hung up. His hand trembled as he replaced the government phone handpiece in the cradle.

Later that night, Ian arrived at Senator Stanifer's apartment at *The Statesmen* apartment building in the foggy bottom area in Washington, D.C. Once the senator had been picked up, Ian introduced himself and apologized and informed him that Director Taylor had to make a last-minute change of plans, there would be no room for additional guests, and besides, The Director wanted to have a frank, open and direct discussion with the senator about their future working relationship. There'd be other opportunities for more relaxed dining in the future should the senator be so inclined.

Senator Stanifer smiled. "Of course, Ian. Let's go meet the old man."

Ian nodded and locked the doors of the vehicle, explaining that you could never be too safe in the D.C. area.

Later that night, Director Taylor watched on a remote screen as the junior senator from Iowa was strapped to a wooden sawhorse. His eyes were covered, a ball gag had been inserted into his mouth, and drool ran from his lips onto the floor. A machine known as the *Sharpshooter* was placed strategically between his now vulnerable anus and not too gently inserted. The night was just getting started for the junior senator from

Iowa. As his screams were muffled by the ball gag, the machine was turned on.

Later after the senator's session with the sharpshooter had ended, he was dragged barely conscious to a device known as the *triangle cross*. His arms and legs were secured to the arms of the metal X-shaped device. A woman approached, wearing a leather mask and nothing else. She brought a metal tray and began to set out a series of curved needles on the tray. She picked up a pair of pliers and spoke to the now trembling and terrified meat strapped to the metal X.

"Hello, my name is 'Pain', and you are about to become acquainted with my specialty. These are carpet needles, each has a purpose, and this is a common pair of pliers. Now don't worry, the needles are sanitary, so there will be no infection, and scarring will be minimal. I'm a professional, after all!  I promise this will be an experience you will remember forever, and you will thank me before it is over. Someone has paid handsomely for you to have this experience, and I intend to make sure they get their money's worth."

Pain removed the leather blindfold from the senator's eyes and insisted he watch her work. She picked up a large curved needle with the pliers. Pulling aside the foreskin from the senator's uncircumcised penis, she pushed the needle slowly through, finally puncturing the skin as the senator's screams continued. She continued until the senator's foreskin, and scrotum were pierced with over a dozen curved needles. As a final added touch, she pierced both of his nipples as well.

Watching from the luxury of his suite, The Director smiled. The lesson was being taught to the junior senator from Iowa with exquisite skill and attention to detail, all of it being recorded and documented. The final touch Pain had promised was delivered.

Senator Stanifer thanked her, clearly speaking the words, "Thank you, Pain, I've enjoyed our session" while the camera recorded his every word. Senator Stanifer had been broken.

Director Taylor made a copy of the entire 'torture date' of Senator Stanifer and then made a shortened version he'd later send to Stanifer himself. Making sure the message was loud and clear, there were copies of the session and his final albeit coerced admission. He'd enjoyed the session.

Ian drove the senator back to his apartment and helped him walk to the elevator.

"May I suggest, sir, that you take a few days off to recover before you return to your duties in the Senate. There's currently a flu virus that has affected many in the area, and that would provide you with a suitable cover while you heal," Ian said matter of factly.

Stanifer nodded, exhausted. "Thank you, Ian."

"My pleasure, sir, and goodnight."

Two weeks later, Director Taylor returned late again for another briefing of the *House Subcommittee on Terrorism, Human Intelligence, Analysis, and Counterintelligence.* The Director was wheeled into the briefing room by Ian and took his place at his usual desk, the usual amenities available. Director Taylor placed a single sheet of scratch paper on the desk and then a pen across the paper. He looked directly at Senator Stanifer, challenging him to repeat his behavior from the last briefing.

Stanifer could not meet The Director's gaze no matter how hard he tried. He stammered and stuttered and finally asked another member of the committee to speak. The briefing continued without incident, and the scratch paper remained mark-free.

After the meeting concluded, Senator Stanifer walked to the elevator a bit gingerly. It would be some time before he healed completely and was able to walk normally. He entered the elevator and turned to see Ron approaching the elevator. He held the door for Ron, and they both rode in absolute silence to the upper chambers of the Senate. The Director replayed the elevator ride, again and again, smiling at the silent results of the sadistic dinner date.

# CHAPTER FIVE

Nick paced back and forth in the room he had set up to study the Shāh Māt files. He needed room, space to move, so he left the room and headed up one of the vehicle access tunnels absent-mindedly wandering, with no particular destination in mind. He stopped, unconsciously. His mind was preoccupied with the files, but the autopilot function of his brain had kicked in and prevented him from walking into the ancient beat up and weathered pickup truck that Diamond Dave had stolen on his way to the facility. The ole girl was an '86 Ford F150. Nick smiled for a moment. He remembered many days spent sitting in the cab of similar F150s driving endless circles around an Alert Aircraft Parking area, or AAP as they were called back then. The planes were loaded with nukes, ridiculously so. Clips of cruise missiles hung from both wings, and the bomb bays were stuffed as well. The theory of mutually assured destruction, or MAD, as a deterrent to war, was taken to the extreme.

Nick ran his hand along the now weathered paint of the metal hood. He felt under the front of the hood and immediately found the hood latch. Muscle memory told him exactly where it was. Then he remembered the hood had to be released from inside the cab, then the secondary latch could be pushed to the left, and the hood would rise. Nick lifted the hood and smiled. The familiar smell of motor oil and sight of the 302-cubic inch motor were welcome sensations. He checked the oil, black and thick, but smelled healthy, no antifreeze in that oil. The dip stick wasn't rusty, that meant the block wasn't cracked. The old girl just needed a little bit of love, some new injectors, and new oil and filter. Maybe an additional fuel filter, air filter, and PCV valve. Hell, maybe even a tune-up, plugs, cap, wires, new water pump, and belts.

Nick closed the hood carefully and then went back to the cab of the truck. He cupped the area around his face as he looked in through the grimy window. The floor of the cab of the truck was eight to twelve inches deep in trash, pop cans, wrappers from candy bars and long ago eaten burgers. Protruding defiantly from the trash were two metal shafts topped by a gear shift knobs, one for the transmission, old girl was a standard transmission, and the second was for the transaxle. She was a 4x4 as well. Diamond Dave knew how to steal a truck. Nick smiled a deep and satisfied smile. He left the vehicle tunnel and went to find Diamond Dave.

Moments later, Nick emerged from the depths of The Hive, as he called the basement of the facility. The team was getting ready for the morning run. Special K would not be joining them yet; she still had a few days to recover from the concussion and broken nose she had suffered from the match with Nick.

Nick asked the group, "Does anyone know where Diamond Dave is?"

"He'll be here in a few. He had to make one last bathroom break before we went out on a run," answered The Mentalist.

"Cool, I'll wait. How far are you going today?" Nick asked.

Bexx answered, "Five miles, *fartlek*, at no less than a six-minute pace." Nick smiled, an intense pace; he liked that Bexx never let up on training, always striving to be better and make the team better, pushing them and herself hard.

"No wonder Diamond Dave had to hit the little boys room, that pace will wake him up, and quick," Nick responded, smiling. Just hearing the pace Bexx would set would've made Diamond Dave need to pee.

When Diamond Dave returned, Nick asked if he could buy the stolen truck from him, offering a couple hundred bucks. Diamond Dave refused the money, saying, "Look man, I just stole it, I don't own it. If you want it, it's yours. It's a piece of shit, ran like shit as well, but I figured it would go unnoticed, fly under the radar if you get my meaning."

Nick nodded to Diamond Dave. "Okay, thanks for the heads up." He smiled and said, "Thanks, man, enjoy the run."

Nick headed back down to the vehicle tunnel and began to inventory the old truck. System by system he went through the truck's mechanical, electrical, and cooling systems. When he was done, he headed to the Bat Cave to access the Web. Parts stores would list their older truck parts on *eBay* and *Amazon*, trying to clear out their older inventory. Thousands of dollars in parts could be had for a fraction of the original cost. Not that the cost mattered to Nick; the team operated off stolen credit card numbers when The Driver was alive, and that hadn't changed.

The first items to purchase and get on their way were the factory service manuals. Once Nick had secured them, he started looking for the long list of parts the ancient truck needed. In the back of his mind, he processed the Shāh Māt files while he scoured the Web for truck parts.

A couple of days later, the parts and service manuals started to arrive at the facility. Boxes large and small, and a sweet set of *Snap-on* hand tools, standard and metric sockets, screwdrivers, allen wrenches, everything Nick might need to begin repairs on the truck. The UPS driver was curious about the sudden increase in deliveries to the facility and mentioned it to Nick.

As he picked up the boxes, Nick smiled and replied cryptically, "Working on a project that's all." Waving as the driver left, Nick was careful as always, never letting out too much information to anyone. There was no telling how deep The Director's Web of informants and spies went. "Just deliver and move on, nosey motherfucker," Nick mumbled under his breath as he began bringing the boxes to the vehicle tunnel entrance. "And tell The Director, I'll be coming soon enough. Tick tock, motherfucker, tick tock." The UPS driver heard none of this and had no idea who The Director was as he continued on his route.

Two days later, Nick was covered in grease and grime from the motor. He pulled off the water pump and prepared to change out the timing chain and made a remarkable discovery. He'd checked the vehicle's speedometer and noted the mileage showed only sixty-eight thousand miles. Most likely, there was an additional one or two hundred thousand miles added to that total. But when Nick accessed the timing chain, he found the gears there were Nylon.

Stunned, he sat back. Talking to himself and smiling he said, "Well, well, you do have some surprises, ole girl." The manufacturer had installed Nylon gears to make the motor quieter when they were initially purchased. They were original equipment and replaced by metal gears later after the first timing chain replacement. This meant the truck had sixty-eight thousand original miles. She was ugly and had been neglect-ed, but she had very little wear on the motor.

Bexx interrupted, "Talking to your truck as if it hears you? And did I hear you call it an old girl?"

Nick crawled out from under the motor and smiled. "Yes! Of course she's a girl. Aren't all vehicles females?"

Bexx shrugged. "I don't know, I've never owned a vehicle. It never seemed practical to purchase one in my current profession."

Nick nodded, wiping the oil off his hands with a rag.

Bexx continued. "We've been together now for how long? Eight months? A year? Do you remember?"

Nick shook his head no. He hadn't really thought about it. He lived day to day. Looking back at anniversary dates seemed pointless. He honestly hadn't expected to be alive this long, and yet he was still here.

"Why do you ask?" he said as he looked at his hands. They hadn't been together for years, but he knew her tone well enough to recognize something in her voice. She was headed somewhere with this line of questioning.

Bexx waited until he looked up at her. "You've been studying the files on The Director and out of nowhere suddenly take an interest in Diamond Dave's stolen truck. The truck has been down here for weeks, and not once did you look at it. A couple of days in the Shāh Māt files, and you become obsessed with the truck. Coincidence? Random event? I seriously doubt it. Care to let me in on the plan? Or is this a Nick se-cret?"

Nick nodded and looked back at his hands. "She has the original timing chain, and the gears are Nylon, which means they haven't been changed out. This motor is nearly new."

Bexx nodded, noticing he had avoided answering her question. "That's good news?" she said, watching him carefully.

He continued on about the motor and other parts he had or would replace, and then finally they both stopped talking. After a few minutes of staring at the engine absently, Nick said, "I don't know why, really. I needed to think and went for a walk and ended up here nearly walking into the truck before I realized it was there. You know how it is for me; I process while I work. I didn't want to destroy my hands splitting another pile of hardwood. So, the truck. Where this will lead? I don't know. I just follow the path. The path led here."

Bexx nodded. "Just keep me in the loop if you can, okay?"

Nick nodded. "I will."

Bexx started to turn and said, "Enjoy your project. Oh, and by the way, Special K is back working out with the team starting today. Not sure how you two are going to mend that relationship, if at all, but heads up; she's up again and out of bed."

Nick nodded, sighed deeply, but said nothing. He just lay back down on the wooden creeper and rolled back under the truck's motor. An hour later, Nick shot out from under the truck's engine and stood up quickly. His eyes were wide open and scanning back and forth as if he were searching for someone in the tunnel.

He then mumbled The Driver's final words, "I will have the last laugh."

# CHAPTER SIX

The team walked up the metal stairway headed towards the kitchen area as a group, noisily laughing and joking among one another. Special K was back, working out, gingerly running in their morning workouts, nursing her broken ribs as she slowly returned to the fitness required for being a member of the team. Bexx watched her progress carefully, making sure she didn't push herself too hard on one hand and making sure she wasn't coddled on the other. Her return to the team would need to be complete. Everyone had to pull their own weight. Special K was no different.

Walking in the back of the group, Bexx listened to the verbal exchange between the team, taking the pulse of the team's mental health and noting they seemed more balanced, even-tempered with Special K's return. As they entered the kitchen, however, Bexx noticed the joking stopped as if a dark cloud had suddenly covered their previously sunny mood. As Bexx walked through the heavy metal door wondering what had happened, she received the answer to her mental question. Nick was sitting in the kitchen, thumbing through the factory repair manuals for the ancient truck he'd adopted from Diamond Dave.

Bexx paused and watched as he continued thumbing through the greasy pages, pretending not to be aware of the team's presence. And even more so, pretending to have no idea of his effect on their mood. The team looked at him warily and then cast careful sideways glances at Special K. It was the first time they had been in a room together since the meltdown in the gym. The team gradually each took a bottle of water or juice from the fridge and sat quietly talking among themselves. Special K sat as well but hadn't retrieved a drink from the fridge. Bexx sat next to Nick and waited, watching as he continued thumbing through the pages. Finally, he looked up and smiled.

"How was the run this morning?" The room was instantly and uncomfortably silent.

Bexx nodded. "It was good. Special K is back working out with us and recovering quickly."

Nick nodded and said, "That's good news."

Bexx waited a moment and asked, "How's the truck repairs coming?"

"Good, really good. There are a few more systems to go through, there's a collector that functions as a switch between the front and rear fuel tank that controls the fuel. Basically, allows the driver to switch from one tank to another in the cab while driving by flipping a switch. It's malfunctioning and needs to be replaced. Then the fuel filters and inline pressure regulator. I already have the fuel injectors replaced, so once all that's done, the fuel system will be like new."

Bexx nodded. She really didn't care about the truck. Nick's obsession with repairing it had given the team a needed break from his unsettling intensity. She admittedly found it intoxicating, but the rest of the team didn't share in that opinion.

Nick smiled and stood up and went to the fridge and took out two cold bottles of smartwater. He opened both and walked to where Special K was seated. Placing one in front of her he said, "Welcome back, glad you're doing so well." Nick placed a hand momentarily on her shoulder and gave her a slight squeeze. He then walked back to where he had left the motor manuals.

The room was silent for several moments, and finally, Special K said, "Thanks, it's good to be back." A slight whistle accompanied each 's' she pronounced due to the freshly missing teeth.

Nick smiled. "We may have to change your name. With that whistle, it reminds me of the cartoon character in *Winnie the Pooh,* the Gopher. Remember when Pooh was having a hard time thinking and Gopher came up through the ground? 'Sssay, whatss wrong, Sssonny?'"

Bexx rolled her eyes. Nick smiled and stared at Special K, waiting for her to reply; she didn't. Nick continued smiling, making the moment more awkward.

Finally, he got up, picked up the motor manuals and began walking to the door. "Have a nice windy day, ladies," he called out, accentuating the whistle and doing his best Gopher imitation.

The door slammed shut, and the room was quiet for several moments after he left. Finally, someone started speaking, and the tension in the room slowly subsided. Nick smiled mischievously as he walked down the stairway to the basement of The Hive.

Svetlana, who was sitting at a table with her sister, jumped up and left the room. She returned a moment later with her laptop and pulled up a YouTube video of the Gopher and Pooh having a discussion about a very windy day. Suddenly, the team was laughing. If Special K was the gopher, then Nick was Pooh, and Pooh at that moment in the video was having a very hard time thinking. The team joked about Nick being an absentminded Pooh working on the truck. Even Bexx laughed at the mental images that came up as they slowly released the tension from the room. However, she knew deep down Nick was up to something. He didn't just randomly appear in the kitchen today for no reason. Everything he did had a purpose.

Nick worked on the fuel system of the truck for the remainder of the day. It was slow going; he was distracted by his memories of the interview of The Driver. Even in his final most pain-filled moments, he was defiant and self-assured he would have the last laugh. He'd defeat Nick, even in death. What did that mean?

Later that night after Nick had cleaned up and reentered the living areas of the missile facility, he lay in bed quietly for some time thinking. Tracing the electrical conduit in the bedroom's concrete ceiling for the thousandth time this week, he finally spoke up.

"Are you awake?"

Bexx lay next to him, eyes open. She wondered if she should answer. The day had been different after he had his gopher whistling exchange with Special K. She was tired. Tired of how difficult it always seemed to be with Nick. He never let up, he couldn't. She understood that now more than ever before. Nick was Nick, damaged, and intense. Maybe more than she was willing to tolerate. Every relationship had a breaking point, and Bexx was approaching hers. She mulled it over, and then she heard herself answer, much to her own surprise.

"Yes, I'm awake."

"When you told me Buffy was worried about me and The Driver - I mean, you told her what we suspected - you asked her to check the hotel in Vegas. Then she found out the two floors of the Bellagio had been reserved, right?"

Bexx closed her eyes. "Yes. Why?"

"Was there anything else? I mean, did she notice anything, or was it a complete surprise? It occurred to me today I never asked you if she had noticed anything independent from us, from me about The Driver. Did she?"

Bexx rolled over. Looking at him, she said nothing for a few moments.

"She told me she had noticed some technical things he had been doing that made no sense. Something to do with the Web and secured access. He had a terminal he shouldn't have needed or wanted. Why do you ask?"

Nick's eyes narrowed. He looked back at the conduit and began tracing it again and again. Lost in thought, he said nothing for several minutes. Bexx had begun to gently doze off when he finally spoke up. She snapped back awake as he spoke.

"Does anyone else know about this except you and her? I mean at the fire that night or since, have you mentioned it to anyone?"

Bexx thought for a moment, trying to understand where he was headed with the question. She tried to remember if she'd mentioned anything Buffy had told her to any of the team.

Eventually, after searching her memories for several moments, she said, "No, I didn't mention it to anyone, and I asked Buffy not to mention it as well. Why do you ask?"

Nick was quiet and then muttered, "Have you mentioned the intelligence files on The Director to anyone?"

Bexx rose up on one elbow, now completely awake. "Where's this going?"

Nick stared directly into her eyes. "Think! Have you mentioned any of this to anyone else on the team?"

Bexx sat up, crossed both legs and thought for a moment. "No! I haven't mentioned any of it to anyone."

Nick sighed deeply. "Good. That's good."

Bexx was puzzled and now admittedly disturbed. She told Nick exactly that and then asked again, "Where are you headed with this?"

Nick sat up on the bed and turned towards Bexx. "You aren't going to like this." And he began to explain what he had mentally uncovered during the truck repairs.

While he talked, Bexx watched him putting the pieces of his latest conspiracy theory into place. When he finally finished, she pulled her hair back with both hands and arms above her head and took a deep breath. She slowly let it out and then stared off in the darkness of their room thinking.

An hour later, she said, "Are you sure?"

Nick nodded. "I think so, but there is only one way to be absolutely sure. Svetlana had emails detailing what The Driver and The Director had planned on doing with any surviving members of the team when they finally defeated us. Was there anyone missing from those plans? Did anyone not get an envelope?"

Bexx thought for a moment. "I don't know. I was so stunned that The Driver had betrayed us, I just handed them out to each team member they concerned. I never thought about checking to see if anyone had been exempt."

Nick nodded. "Exactly. What is missing matters again. Let's have Svetlana compile them again. And while she's doing that, ask Buffy to talk to me privately. I need to learn more about these backdoor communications The Driver had and shouldn't have. Agreed?"

Bexx nodded. "So, we're back in this mess again?"

Nick nodded grimly. "Yes, actually it's the same damn mess."

Bexx lay down. "This is exhausting. How do you do this, day after day?"

Nick shook his head slowly. Eyes closed, he whispered, "Until I met you, this is all I've ever known. Scheming, conniving pieces of shit were a constant. Guess that's why I'm able to survive our Director. A lifetime of practice."

# CHAPTER SEVEN

Nick spent the next morning finishing the fuel system overhaul on the thirty plus-year-old truck. When he finished, he made a short detour into the Bat Cave to see Buffy and Svetlana. When he arrived, Bexx was already there. She was asking Svetlana to reexamine the email trails between The Driver and The Director, asking her to look for anything unusual. Nick and Bexx had made a decision to leave the search open-ended rather than tell Svetlana what to look for. They chose to have her look for anything at all out of place and see what might turn up. When the search was completed, Svetlana was to make copies of what she found and bring them to Bexx. Meanwhile, Nick asked Buffy to step outside and walk with him to the far end of the fenced area around the facility.

Buffy asked, "What's up now?"

"Sorry for all the cloak and dagger lately. I need you to explain to me what it was that made you think The Driver was working against us. Bexx said you suspected something even before I figured it out."

"Well, the final issue that sealed it was when he showed me a new VSAT terminal he had acquired. It could only be used to communicate with a secure system called Skynet. It is military grade, very secure, very traceable. He had no need for it. If anything, it was a risk to have at all. He had no idea I've worked the civilian VSAT systems for years. I never told him, so when he told me about it and tried to pretend it would be a great asset, I knew he was against us."

Nick nodded. It made sense. "So where is this military-grade VSAT now?"

"On the rooftop of the facility where he installed all the VSAT equipment. I haven't needed to go back up there, so I left it alone."

"Does anyone else know about the VSAT systems on the team? I mean, you are the team expert, is there a backup to you in case of emergency?"

"Yes, we always train others in case of emergency. Redundancy is a requirement in our line of work. I'm sure you're aware of that concept."

Nick nodded. All military teams trained in depth, keeping a primary and alternate in each specialty. To avoid a single point of failure was critical in tactical operations of any kind.

"So, who else on the team is at least familiar with the systems?"

"Well, I'm the primary. Special K is the alternate. With her language training, she was the natural fit, and then The Mentalist is her back up."

"Anyone else?"

"No, that's it. We're a small team. Two alternates seemed to be enough."

Nick nodded.

"Why do you ask? Why couldn't you ask me in front of Svetlana and Bexx?"

"I don't know, probably just me being paranoid, but I think we still need to compartmentalize this. Like the Shāh Māt files, we need to keep this all close to the vest. I'm honestly not sure why. It's just a feeling. Speaking of the Shāh Māt files, how did you find them? Was there anything unusual about them? Or how you found them? It was you who found them, right?"

"Yes, I found them. Unusual? Hmm, I don't know. It did seem odd that they were alone in a subfile. And the size of them, I assumed they would be loaded with pictures. The files' size was enormous for being primarily text."

"Was the system difficult to get into? I mean, did it seem more or less difficult or the same as usual?"

"Pretty much the same as usual. It wasn't particularly difficult. I was worried I'd been in the system too long. I was about to leave, and then there was the Shāh Māt file. Come to think of it, not only was it alone, in its own folder, it was named. Most of the files were assigned a serial number."

Nick nodded. "Okay, thanks, that helps, the file itself is unusual. It was extremely detailed. The Director being who he is, and what he is, made the existence of the file alone suspicious. Had he known of its existence, he would've destroyed it immediately." Logically, someone else had compiled it, then uploaded it. This kind of information should've been kept locked up in a safe, hard copies only…unless someone wanted it found. But who? Who would go to all the effort of compiling this kind of detailed information and then make it electronic and accessible to any world-class hacker? Nick said none of this to Buffy.

"Do you think you could access the system you found the Shāh Māt files on again?"

"Definitely, yes. Why?"

"I want to see the file system. Understand what you are describing with my own eyes. Can you do it now?"

"Sure, let's go back to the Bat Cave. It may take a few minutes, but I can get back in."

Nick nodded, and they turned and began walking back to the facility. Once they were inside the Bat Cave, Buffy hacked her way back into the top-secret STATEROOM system. She explained to Nick as she navigated the back door into the software that The Driver liked to use brute force to compromise a system and gain entry. Her methods were more subtle and delicate. Nick laughed. It made sense. The Driver always bragged about his ability to violate and pillage the Web and hack systems using his alleged sexual prowess. To him, every hack was a conquest.

Buffy spent a few minutes looking around the files and finally said, "It's gone, the file Shāh Māt. It isn't there anymore. It was a subfile of this file. I specifically looked into this file last, and it was there; now it's been removed or deleted."

Nick said nothing. It all made sense. No one would leave a file like that on an electronic system for long. They had to know that the system had been compromised and exactly what files had been accessed.

While Nick had been speaking with Buffy, Bexx had asked Svetlana for the email search and left the Bat Cave. She watched Nick and Buffy from the facility doorway. Again, she heard the familiar gait of Special K walking up from behind her.

"What is it now?" Special K asked. "Aliens from Roswell infiltrating us?"

Bexx smirked. "No, not aliens. Just the usual Nick has a 'feeling.' I've learned to trust his feelings even if they are exhausting. I have to admit, I'm a bit exhausted by this whole Director grudge match thing."

"Yes, well, we all are. At least back in Ukraine, our missions were relatively simple. We were tasked, then we completed that task and waited for the next one. This is never-ending. Has the thought ever occurred to you what we'll do if and when Nick and The Director finally do meet? What if Nick survives or somehow wins? What will he do then? You do realize this is who he is. Who he was before The Director crossed his path. He was waiting for the next enemy to attack. He chose to enter Baroota thinking he was going after human traffickers. Bexx, this is who he is."

"And your point is?"

"Why can't we just go back to the way it was? Nick doesn't work well with us, with any of us. Do you realize that? We train and train, but in the end, Nick comes up with the solution, not us. Before Nick, we worked together. Now we wait to see what falls out of Nick's ass this week."

"What would you suggest?" Bexx asked quietly.

Special K stepped closer. "I suggest we go back to working as a team. I suggest you consider giving that another chance." Special K placed a hand on Bexx's waist.

"By going back to working as a team, do you mean the entire team? Or do you mean you and me?"

"I mean both," Special K replied. She removed her hand and turned and walked away.

Bexx said nothing and continued to watch Nick and Buffy as they talked. They turned and began to walk back towards the facility. She allowed the door to close and walked back into the facility.

# CHAPTER EIGHT

W hile Bexx watched Nick and Buffy through the partially opened door, Svetlana stared at her computer screen. It was pretty obvious Nick was on to something. Once again, they were compartmentalizing. Bexx spoke to her while Buffy and Nick went on a little stroll around the facility fence line. Nothing obvious about that. She thought about the way Bexx had framed the request she had made.

*"Take another look at the emails between The Driver and The Director and let me know what you find, print them all out again and organize them and let me know when you're done."*

Ambiguous at best. They were on to something and once again had no idea who they could trust. Shake the tree and see what falls out, that was how Nick put it in the past. They were shaking the tree again. What had she missed? What had he seen? Svetlana stared a few more minutes, thinking back to the email trail she had found and how she had organized it. There was nothing there she could see that would bring Nick back to this level of caution. She sighed deeply and began the search again. She cross-referenced each email thread that referenced a team member and what The Driver and Director had planned for them when Nick was finally defeated. Interesting now that she looked back, Nick had no after plan in The Director's grand scheme. His death was unquestionably a requirement. The rest of the team, however, had a lifetime of slavery and prostitution awaiting them. Except for The Driver, of course; he would survive by hiding in plain sight as he always had, Buffy would be his property and maybe one or two others until he grew tired of them. Funny, she thought back to the surprised look on his face when she began her attack, and a grim satisfaction warmed her thoughts. The shocked look on The Driver's face when she dropped him would be a memory she would cherish for a very long time. Svetlana continued the search while Buffy returned to the Bat Cave.

"Interesting day?" Svetlana asked.

"Yes, I suppose," Buffy answered, "just another day in the Bat Cave."

"What is it this time? Obviously, they tasked you with something. I've been tasked to go back through the email threads between The Driver and The Director and look for anything out of the ordinary. How about you?"

Buffy replied, "Oh, nothing that interesting. Nick just wanted to know what made me think The Driver was working against us. What was it exactly that made me suspicious."

"So what was it?"

"Nothing in particular, really. It just all started to feel weird, the comments he made, things that didn't add up. You know, woman's intuition. Men are simple, they aren't capable of hiding much for very long." Buffy smiled.

Svetlana nodded yes and smiled but said nothing.

When Nick was satisfied he understood what had caused Buffy to doubt The Driver, he asked one final question, "Does this VSAT terminal have internal memory?"

"Yes, it does."

"How large is the memory?"

"One terabyte. The entire system is self-contained. The military and civilian systems are made to be mobile. There is an internal server in the system itself. The entire system is accessed by a standard keyboard with standard military security requirements. Login name, twelve to sixteen letter password that requires two uppercase letters and two special characters. The system is on the roof of the facility and is contained in several metal containers that are similar to metal suitcases. To access the keyboard, you pull out a tray that has a pop-up screen and internal keyboard."

Nick grimaced. "Password? Really? Damn it! The Driver is dead. How would we know what his password would have been? It could have been anything, like 'TheDriverishung@donky$long12.'"

Buffy laughed out loud. "Well, yes that could have been a password option, but he was very simple in his password creation. I know what the password is to access that system. He made a point out of repeating it out loud every time he logged in. I was stunned when he spoke it out loud."

Nick stared at her, eyes wide open. "Seriously? You know the password?"

"Of course."

"Okay, could you show me now exactly where the military grade system is and how to access the keyboard? When we're done, never go up there again, and don't mention this to anyone."

"Sure. I can do that. Can I ask why?"

"Sure, you can ask." Nick smiled but didn't answer.

Buffy nodded. "I get it; don't ask, don't tell."

When Buffy and Nick arrived on the rooftop, Nick asked her to step back for a moment and then he took a picture of the entire VSAT set up with his cell phone. Buffy was curious why but didn't ask. Then when he was sure he had enough pictures of the system, she began to explain it to him.

Nick sat on the rooftop for several hours after Buffy had gone back down to the Bat Cave. He accessed the internal memory of the military grade VSAT and began to look through the message log timeline. What he saw there stopped him cold. His vision collapsed into a dark tunnel momentarily, tunnel vision. He recognized it immediately. The body reacted to a threat by dropping adrenaline into the bloodstream. Preparing for flight or fight. Nick, having been through multiple fights for survival, dropped into fight mode almost instantly at the slightest unexpected event. He'd hoped when he accessed the VSAT memory, he'd be able to gain some insight into what The Driver had meant when he said he would have the last laugh. What he found was exactly that and nothing he expected.

Nick swore under his breath. Several deep breaths later, he was still shaking. Trying to read the last message recorded in the memory log, he could barely make sense of the words. The tremendous adrenaline dump combined with the shock of what was written there made his cognitive abilities diminish significantly. The words were there in front of him in plain English, but suddenly he couldn't understand them; they were just random symbols. Meaningless. He might as well be trying to read the computer screens on the *Nebuchadnezzar* in *The Matrix*.

When Nick finally came back down from the shock of what he found, he was able to read and comprehend the messages. After he'd read enough to understand exactly what The Driver's final words had meant, he put the VSAT system back in exactly the same position it had been before using the picture on his cell phone to make sure it was identical. He climbed down the metal ladder that allowed access to the rooftop and retreated to the tunnels in the facility. He returned to the ancient Ford truck. Opening the hood, he mentally walked his mind through each of the vehicle's mechanical and electrical systems. Step by step, part by part. Slowing his breathing, Nick returned to work on the ancient truck.

Later that night, Nick explained to Bexx what he had found on the facility's rooftop. Speaking in barely discernable whispers, he detailed everything he had read. Bexx was silent, staring wide-eyed at him.

"Are you sure? Absolutely sure?"

Nick nodded, they spoke for a few more minutes, and then Bexx let out a loud, frustrated yell and erupted from their bedroom in a wild fury. As she slammed the door and walked to the TV room, several of the Asgarda were there playing cards. They stopped and asked if Bexx was okay.

"Okay? Do I look okay? Jesus, I'm tired of this shit! Conspiracy theories every goddamn day! Who can live like this?" Bexx paced back and forth for a moment and then left to go to the kitchen. "Sorry, ignore me, just a minor meltdown," she muttered angrily as she walked off. The Asgarda all looked at each other, exchanging silent glances. Nick's paranoid personality was finally getting on her nerves.

Once Bexx arrived in the kitchen area, she took a bottle of water from the fridge and opened it. She paused, looking at the floor and seeing nothing. Breathing deeply, she finally began to drink. Would this ever be over?

At that same moment, The Messenger arrived at the steel door, pushed the buzzer and waited for the red light to turn green. The light changed colors, and the electronic lock released. The Messenger opened the door. After taking a couple of steps inside, he let the door close and then waited for his eyes to adjust to the darkness. When he could start to see shapes of the office furniture, he approached the silhouette sitting at the desk. He waited momentarily as the shape sat back and motioned for him to begin his briefing.

"You asked to be notified of any events involving the Shāh Māt files. Our hacker friend has again attempted to locate them, using the same tools in the previous hack and again leaving the hacking pattern we discovered during the last breach. I had the files removed as you asked, so nothing new was gained in this attempt."

The silhouette nodded.

"Additionally, the VSAT terminal that had been silent was turned back on today, no messages were sent. But the unit's memory was accessed, several messages were read. Would you like me to shut down the terminal remotely?"

No! The Silhouette shook its head adamantly, then a hand reached forward and pulled a pad of legal-sized yellow paper to the center of the desk. The Messenger heard the furious scratches of the pen marking the paper urgently. The page was torn off and then pushed forward toward The Messenger. A hand motion indicated he was to read it immediately and out loud.

"Leave it all alone, touch nothing! Brief me of any activity on the

VSAT immediately!" The Messenger spoke calmly and then replied quietly but firmly, "Of course!"

The Messenger was dismissed with a silent wave of the hand and exited the darkroom, making his way towards the large metal door.

# CHAPTER NINE

Nick sat silently in the darkness as the rooftop of the facility was hammered by the North Dakota winds. He found a place where he could watch the VSAT terminal and still be somewhat protected from the persistent blowing wind. It had been three days since he had found the messages the VSAT memory files held. Three nights of sitting in the dark, waiting for the person who sent the messages to return. In the past three days, his relationship with Bexx had deteriorated rapidly. He'd moved out of the room they shared in a very public fight. It was very clear to everyone in the facility they were over. The relationship ended. Bexx had had enough of the constant stress of his conspiracy theories and then added to anyone who asked, Nick had started secretly drinking. She was done and made that clear to everyone. She spent most of her time with the team training and avoiding Nick, which was fine with him. It gave him more time to plan and repair the truck.

Nick threw himself at the truck with renewed enthusiasm, working some days for fourteen hours straight, only stopping to eat and return to the rooftop and wait for whoever had sent the messages to finally show their face. Several nights, he fell asleep in the darkness and awoke hours later when the sun began to rise and warm the facility rooftop. He started to enjoy the peace of being on the rooftop; the quiet and solitude made him realize the presence of the team had become a distraction. The constant noise and irritating sound of the language they all spoke kept him off his game. The rooftop became a place he could hide and think without the suspicious side glances and quiet whispers of the team as they waited for the next shoe to drop in the Bexx and Nick reality show.

While Nick was enjoying his self-imposed exile from the team, Bexx had received the emails from Svetlana and gone through them. There was nothing in them to suggest anything wrong with her team. She talked the contents over with Svetlana and asked her for her opinion.

"Do you see anything here? Anything at all?" Bexx asked.

"No. I looked through them, and they seem consistent. Everyone who survived, if they survived either Cachibaché or Izadi, had a future in

The Director's world. A very grim future. The only clear message in any of these messages is that Nick had no future, and apparently neither did Nõn. It seems clear from the earlier messages between The Director and The Driver, Nick and Nõn were going to die no matter what their plans for the outcome for the rest of the team."

Bexx was momentarily quiet as she remembered the day The Sniper had opened fire on them, vaporizing Nõn's head and nearly killing Nick as well. Then Bexx remembered the sound of Nick grunting as he began to get up. Her eyes closed as the brutal memories returned.

"Bexx?" Svetlana spoke her name apprehensively.

"Yes, sorry, just remembering something I'd rather not. So back to the emails. Have you uncovered anything new? Any new messages that had nothing to do with the team or Nick?"

"No, nothing new. I did a pretty deep and exhausting search and found nothing new."

Bexx nodded. "Okay, probably just a wild ass shot in the dark. Nick was sure there'd be something here."

"I can look at them again. I mean, he does have a remarkable gift in seeing what others miss."

Bexx shook her head no. "No, I'd rather not open up that can of worms. Let's let it rest for now. I'd rather not feed his paranoia." Bexx raised her eyebrows and looked at Svetlana with a sarcastic smirk.

"Understood. So where has Nick been lately? I know the facility is big, but he seems to have disappeared since." Svetlana stopped.

"Since? Since we broke up, you mean. Since he moved out of my room? Who knows, drinking? Drunk asleep in a corner somewhere? I don't know, and I don't care. I'm done trying to manage Nick."

"Yes, sorry, didn't mean to bring up such a sensitive subject."

"No worries. We're all adults here..., er, I mean, he is an adult, sort of. But I'm fine, moving on. Live and learn."

"No chance of that being repairable?"

"I'd think not. Just trying to decide what to do next. Really, I'm relieved he's stayed out of everyone's way. It makes my role here much easier. I can't manage the boy/man Nick is and the entire team. It was pretty obvious something would have to give eventually."

Svetlana nodded but said nothing.

On the seventh day of Nick's rooftop exile, he'd been sitting quietly in the dark again, armed as usual with his favorite .45 caliber *Para Ordinance GI Expert.* He was listening to the sound of the wind as it raced across the flat fields that surrounded the missile facility. His mind began to wander, imagining what it would be like to ride the wind until it stopped. Where would he end up? Did the wind ever really stop? He hadn't thought about it. What if it didn't? What if this exact gust of wind traveled across these fields and the entire state, making its way eventually to the Atlantic? Or maybe it turned and crossed into Canada. Wind had no rules. Wind did what it was made to do, and no one questioned it, no one looked at the wind and asked, "Why are you the way you are?" Suddenly, Nick snapped back to the rooftop. He heard a noise, slight, faint, the sound of someone climbing the metal ladder to the rooftop. The sound was complicated, at first it sounded like the ladder would have sounded had a person been carefully climbing, then the cadence changed. Nick's heart rate rose, as did his breathing, about time his surveillance paid off and the person who'd sent the messages would be caught. Bexx would see he was right, and maybe he could salvage their relationship.

Nick waited, coiled in the darkness, the *Para Ordinance* waiting to come to life. Nick quietly clicked the safety off as a dark figure quietly rose above the roof line, head first, then shoulders. The figure paused, then the entire body was silhouetted in the darkness. Nick watched as the figure stood on the rooftop, silently scanning the darkness like a predator looking for any sign of danger. Eventually, the figure relaxed and walked directly to the VSAT terminal. As the terminal came to life and the figure typed in The Driver's password, Nick was slowly rising to his feet, the

*Para Ordinance* begging his finger to compress the competition trigger and unleash his fury. He was about to do just that when a second figure appeared on the ladder. Nick froze. Two? There were two of them?

The second figure cleared the metal ladder and approached the VSAT terminal. They whispered to each other in Russian as the first figure logged in and began to type the next message to The Director.

*Plan in motion, N&B have split. N is more isolated than ever, drinking heavily, staying in the tunnels under the facility. Should be able to push him to breaking point soon. Advise.*

A few moments later, a reply to the messages was received on the VSAT. Nick watched as the two shadows read the message and then replied. The VSAT was closed, and the rooftop was dark again. The two figures whispered to each other as they carefully and quietly made their way back to the metal ladder and began to climb down from the rooftop.

For a moment, Nick considered killing them both. Quick and clean, bullet to the back of the head of the one who would get on the ladder last, then drop the next one while still trapped on the ladder, two clean head shots and done. Nick smiled at the idea of catching them unaware and killing them. Seeing the horror and fear in their eyes in those final moments, realizing their worst fear had been brought to life. But he stopped. Why he wasn't sure at first. Then the path forward became clear. It was time, time to set the final plan in motion. Nick waited, putting the Para reluctantly back on safe. He returned to the VSAT terminal, logged in and pulled up the memory files and began to read the messages from tonight's exchange. When he was done, he closed the terminal and then checked to make sure no one was outside the facility before he began to climb down the metal ladder.

Two days later, Nick was satisfied that the ancient F150 was ready. At least ready for a test run. Time to check out all the system repairs he had completed and see if there were any he had missed. Nick got in and inserted the double-sided key into the ignition and turned the key. The new ignition switch carried the current from the battery to the starter relay and then on the starter motor. The starter motor began to spin, and the F150 roared to life. Like *Optimus Prime* receiving the gift of the

"Allspark," the truck had a new lease on life.

Exhaust flowed from the *Magnaflow* mufflers as the engine now rolled happily in a deep, throaty purr. Nick smiled a proud smile. He got out of the truck and opened the vehicle tunnel blast doors. Moments later, the reincarnated truck ejected from the tunnel like *The General Lee* in a *Dukes of Hazard* testosterone-laden moment. Only the signature horn blast of The General was missing. Nick headed to the gate and then out onto the open road.

# CHAPTER TEN

The next night was movie night for the Asgarda. Nick smiled as he listened to the team settle into the entertainment area of the facility. Finally, he saw an impact he was having on the team's daily routine that didn't include anxiety and mayhem. Nick listened as the movie was loaded and the team took their individual places, some lounging on couches, others lying on the floor, heads propped up on pillows.

Nick quietly entered the room and watched from the back, trying to be as unobtrusive as he could. He noticed Bexx wasn't present in the room. They hadn't spoken in several days. To be honest, they hadn't even made eye contact. They were like planets in orbit around the same sun but never crossing paths, separated by a distance too great to close. No matter, this would all be over soon. Nick had made his mind up, waiting now. Poised to step into the final confrontation with The Director, he had one final piece of the puzzle to put into place. The feeling was overwhelming and at the same time a relief. With Bexx no longer in the equation and the team on the sidelines with her, Nick was free to act alone and unencumbered by the burden of the what-ifs of the team's involvement.

The movie was a *Guy Ritchie* masterpiece, *Sherlock Holmes, A Game of Shadows*. One of Nick's favorites. *Robert Downey Jr.* was on point in nearly every movie he made since rehab. The fact that he had bounced back so well and maintained his life gave Nick hope as well. Maybe after The Director was defeated, life could go on. Nick smiled and shook his head, best not to get too far ahead of himself. The Director wouldn't just roll over and die because Nick showed up. Quite the opposite. Nick would have to surprise him in a way he'd never expect. That would be difficult given the recent revelation that at least two of the Asgarda were secretly communicating with him on the VSAT system. Nick had an idea of who they were, but the reality hit him that letting them continue would be an unexpected move The Director would never see coming. They had and would continue to feed information to The Director. That was definitely an exploitable option.

While Nick and the team watched the movie, Bexx sat in her room reading. The absolute quiet and safety of the missile facility was a comfort, but one she knew would be ending very soon. It was time to move on. She hadn't made any definite plans yet, but after talking with the rest of the team, specifically Svetlana and Special K, it became apparent the time for a change was here. There was a soft knock at the door, and she stopped reading and listened. The knock came again, this time louder and more urgent.

"Yes?"

"May I come in?" she heard The Mentalist ask.

Bexx closed the book she was reading and opened the door. "What is it?" She could tell from the look on The Mentalist's face something was wrong.

"I hate to ask this. I know things have changed, and you and Nick are no longer together, but..."

"But what?"

"I already asked JT, and he said to leave Nick alone. Whatever he was doing, there was a purpose for it. He absolutely refuses to talk to Nick."

Bexx rolled her eyes and sighed heavily. "What's Nick doing now?"

"We were watching a movie, the entire team, just relaxing for a moment, and Nick was there I guess. Suddenly, he yelled, 'That's it!' We all jumped; we weren't aware he was there with us. He walked over and picked up the remote for the Blu-ray player and rewound the movie to the beginning of a scene. He's watched it now three times. He just keeps replaying it and mumbling to himself under his breath. I thought maybe before we have another one of Nick's meltdowns and he goes off and dismembers someone, you could come and..."

Bexx put her head down and glared at the floor for a moment, "All right, get everyone out of the room. I'll go speak to him."

"Already done. Everyone left immediately. Nick is still in there alone, replaying that one scene in the movie we were watching."

Bexx nodded, took a deep breath, and smiled at The Mentalist. "One last time! Off to babysit."

Bexx found Nick exactly as The Mentalist had described him. Sitting in the entertainment area of the facility, watching the movie the team had been watching. Bexx didn't recognize the movie; she watched very little television and fewer movies. She sat back and watched the scene Nick was replaying over and over. Sherlock was in a castle in Switzerland after being severely injured to gain the intel into his archenemy Professor Moriarty. He had chosen to meet Moriarty in a game of chess on an exterior balcony of the castle. Each player moved their pieces on the board while simultaneously they played a more serious game inside the castle to either start a war or avoid one.

Sherlock won the inside game and then advised Moriarty he was also dismantling his criminal empire. Moriarty would be financially ruined. Sherlock had won the day, but Moriarty promised he would destroy Dr. Watson and his new wife's lives. Holmes then had to make a choice to ultimately defeat Moriarty. He had to do something totally unpredictable. Moriarty understood his logic and methods too well. Holmes pulled him over the balcony brick wall, and they fell into the water far below.

Nick replayed the scene again and watched intently, focusing on every movement, every nuance, nodding occasionally.

Bexx sat next to him, slowly easing into the space next to him. She whispered, "Nick?"

Nothing.

Louder now, "Nick!"

Nick jumped, disoriented. He leaned away from her, looking dazed, and didn't recognize her at first. They hadn't been this close in a very long time.

Finally, he said, "Hey, where did you come from?"

Bexx smiled. "My room! Apparently, you took over the television and were acting odd for most people, but normal for you. The Mentalist came to get me to rein you in."

Nick nodded and began to play the scene again. "Look at this, this is it, exactly what I needed to see. I've been racking my brain trying to find a way to defeat The Director - and BAM, this comes up out of nowhere. I can't tell you how many times I've watched this scene and never really paid attention. Today it was like I saw it for the first time. Damn it! This has been in front of my face the entire time, and I missed it."

Bexx nodded; Nick was in a manic moment, that much was obvious.

Bexx watched the scene with Nick, and then when he replayed it again, she said, "Well, I see that this means something to you. So as long as you're okay and not about to eviscerate one of my team, I'll let you be."

Nick just nodded silently and continued to watch the scene again.

Bexx rolled her eyes and groaned. Lifting up her arms up in frustration, she left the room, disgusted.

A couple of hours later, Nick finally stopped watching the scene and turned off the television. He sat in silence, staring at the concrete wall, motionless. Now he understood what he needed to do. There could be no plan; he would have to be spontaneous. Do something unpredictable The Director would never see coming, something simple, and yet so deadly effective.

Nick walked to a nearby desk and began to write.

When Nick finished the first letter, he sealed it in an envelope and put a number one on the envelope. He then began another letter; it took more time to write, and when he was done, he was drained. It was time to go. He knew that now. Not tonight, tonight he would need to sleep and pack some clothes. Tomorrow, though, the final confrontation with The Director would begin.

The next day, Nick woke up early and headed to the facility gym. JT was up and going through his own workout when Nick entered. JT stopped rocking the speed bag as Nick approached. It was clear in the purposeful movement Nick was there for a reason.

"Wassup, bradah? You look like you have something serious on your mind."

"Coming to say goodbye, gotta go handle this shit. The time is now."

"You need me to come along? Watch your back?"

"Nope, I got this. What I need is for you to keep an eye on the girls, bro. Not everyone here is on the same page. Me and Bexx are split, and the team is aware of that. Keep your eyes open, okay?"

"Sure thing, bradah! To be honest, I'm thinking about going back to the islands. Been too long since I saw the homeland. No offense to the team, but really, I feel it's time to go as well. Svetlana has made me some papers that will get me home, a passport, identification and a bank account loaded with stacks. I'll be going soon as well."

"Cool, sounds good. I do need a favor though before you leave. Sometime today or tomorrow, someone will realize I've left. When the word gets out, quietly mention to Bexx that we talked and I left an envelope in the top drawer of her dresser explaining everything."

"That's it? Envelope, top drawer. Nothing else?"

"That's it."

"Got it, consider it done. what's your plan, bradah? How you gonna ghost this prick?"

"No plan, that's the plan. Planning hasn't worked yet. Somehow, he anticipates my every move. So, no plan is the best plan, if that makes sense."

JT nodded. "It does, and it doesn't. Go with the flow, I guess is what I'm hearing."

"Exactly."

Nick turned and began to walk away. "Be good, JT. Thanks for your help."

JT watched Nick leave and returned to the speed bag, his hands moving so fast there was nothing but a blur.

Nick walked down the vehicle tunnel to the ancient but now rebuilt F150. He had packed light, no shower, no shave. His backpack contained the Shāh Māt files and a change of clothes. He threw the backpack across the front seat and jumped in the truck. Slamming the door, he started the truck and pulled slowly out of the facility. First stop, Grand Forks. Ole girl needed new shoes, then the restore would be complete. After the tires were installed, it was on to meet The Director.

# CHAPTER ELEVEN

Nick pulled the F150 into *Big Jim's Eastside Tires* at 111 Gateway Drive and paid for a set of tires, mounted and balanced. The final step in the ole girl's facelift would be complete in a few hours, so he waited in the waiting room and watched daytime television for the first time in many years. There were two women waiting as well. One was older, sixty to sixty-five, and she sat reading a book and didn't look up to acknowledge Nick had sat down. The second woman was younger, maybe thirty-five, and a nervous wreck. She sat and fidgeted, crossing and uncrossing her legs, checking her cell phone periodically for messages. Finally, she got up and asked one of the people at the counter for a piece of paper and a pen. She came back to the waiting area and wrote a quick note.

*Meet at the parking garage at noon?* She drew a smiley face, and then as an afterthought, she wrote *I will make it worth your while, I promise.*

She folded the note and then returned the pen to the counter, thanking them much too enthusiastically. Then she walked out to her car and placed the note on the center console.

Nick watched as she walked out to her car and then returned without the note. She smiled at him as she returned. He raised his eyebrows but said nothing. He looked at her hand; no wedding ring, and no sign she had been wearing one ever. It was evident from her nervous behavior she was hiding something.

Nick sighed and pretended to pay attention to the daytime TV drivel. How anyone could watch this crap day after day and not experience severe brain damage was unimaginable. The latest daytime chef sensation was preparing a pasta dish while explaining to the token celebrity guest the finer points of preparing the dish. One of the steps involved pouring a quarter cup of vodka into the pan and then lighting it. A large blue flame erupted from the pan, and the audience all let out the required mindless "Ohhhh" at the sight of the now flaming pan. The cameraman panned the audience to get the people's reaction to the stunt. Nick grimaced as the severely overweight audience members clapped mindlessly.

He thought silently, *who knew getting tires could be such an aggravation?*

Out of the corner of his eye, he saw the mechanic grab the keys to the nervous woman's car and then walk out of the business and open the car door. He stopped for a minute and read the note. He then started the car and drove it into the bay. A few moments later, he returned and told his boss he would be taking a second lunch, which meant he would be working until noon. He said this loud enough that the nervous woman heard him. She smiled. Nick yawned and hoped his truck's tires would be installed before the amateurish booty call was being consummated. Five-minutes later, the nervous woman made a phone call, making sure everyone in the tire store could hear her.

"Hi, hon, how's your day been? That's good! I'm at the tire store, and it's going to be a while. Probably won't be home until one or so. Just wanted to let you know, so you didn't worry. Yes, they are very busy. No, I'm fine. I'll just wait here, thanks. Maybe we could take the kids out for dinner tonight? That would be great, love you too."

*Somewhere, some dumb bastard believed this woman gave a shit about him,* Nick thought. *Been there, done that. It's a rude awakening to find out your woman has a garbage disposal for a soul. Bitch lined me up to die in Panama, and I never even saw it coming.*

Nick got up and moved away from the nervous woman. Too much reality for a simple tire install.

*Love you too,* Nick thought. His eyes hardened. Love you too, how many times had he heard that line of shit roll off some woman's tongue? It meant nothing to any of them. It was like a post-hypnotic suggestion left in every man's mind at age twelve. Hear these three words, and your critical thinking skills go to shit. Anyone who believed in love probably still believed in the Tooth Fairy and Santa Claus. Reality wasn't something most people could handle.

An hour later, the booty call mechanic returned and placed the keys to Nick's truck on the counter. Nick got up and went to pay for the tires with one of the stolen credit card accounts The Driver had set up. He saw the mechanic's name on his shirt, Matt.

*Matt, the playboy mechanic. Good luck with Libby Hatch, the psychotic two timing housewife.* Nick thought as his receipt was printing up and the salesperson explained the tire warranty. Nick doubted the warranty would ever be needed; his chances of being alive a week from now were slim at best. He ran through all the possible outcomes and realized this was a one-way trip. Might as well enjoy the ride. The clock was ticking.

While Nick was driving out of the parking lot at *Big Jim's Eastside Tires,* Bexx had just realized he wasn't in the facility. She had gone to the vehicle tunnel entrance and found the F150 was gone. She checked the rest of the facility and found no sign of Nick.

Bexx checked in at JT's gym and looked around for Nick while the team was being put through the paces of the latest grueling workout JT had dreamed up. When he stopped, she asked, "Have you seen Nick?"

JT looked at her for a moment and then told the team, "Take five, get some water and keep moving."

JT motioned to Bexx to follow him, and they walked off out of the team's immediate presence.

"Nick is gone."

Bexx spoke loudly, "What do you mean he's gone? Gone where?"

JT spoke even more quietly. "He left this morning, took the truck and said he had some business to take care of. I think he's gone to face The Director. He said he had to do this solo. That he couldn't risk you or the team."

Bexx was angry. "So, he just left?" she yelled. "No good luck, goodbye, nothing? Just running off on some testosterone contest with The

Director?"

JT nodded. "There's more. He asked me to tell you he left an envelope for you in your dresser."

"Oh, he left a note? Wonderful. Anything else I need to know while we're at it?"

JT thought for a moment; might as well get it all out now. "I'm going to be leaving as well. I'm going home. It's been too long since I was on the island. It has been an honor to train your team and be associated with your cause, but this is not my path. Hopefully, we learned something from each other, and we can part better for knowing each other." He reached out his hand to shake Bexx's hand.

Bexx paused; she was angry Nick had left without a word. But she calmed down and shook JT's hand and nodded. "Thank you for telling me, and good luck."

Bexx turned and left the gym and went straight to her room to retrieve the envelope from her dresser drawer. When she opened the drawer, she found two envelopes. She took them out and opened the one with her name on it.

*Bexx, sorry how things have turned out. I would've liked to speak to you in person, but since we haven't spoken in several days, that seemed to be pointless. I'm going to meet The Director in person. The Shāh Māt files have provided me a way to end this. I won't have a better time than now to bring closure to this nightmare, and I can't bring you into it. Probably best this way. Nick*

Bexx put down the first letter and opened the second letter. She read it and then let out a breath.

"What?" she whispered, astonished.

She reread the letter again to make sure she hadn't misunderstood what Nick had written. When she was done, she crushed the letter and then went outside the facility to burn it.

Later that night, Bexx called a meeting and asked Special K to start a fire. When everyone was gathered around, she handed the letter to Special K and asked her to pass it around when she was done. When everyone had read Nick's letter to her, she began.

"We're leaving the facility. I won't be a part of this any longer. Anyone who wishes may follow me. Nick has left on a suicide mission, and I think it's best if we all just cut our losses. Does anyone have questions? Comments?"

There were none.

Bexx nodded to Diamond Dave. "You're welcome to stay with the team if you'd like to."

Dave said, "Thanks, I'll consider it." He had no intention of staying with the team. They would be much too big a target if the death match between Nick and The Director went south and Nick lost. Dave would go solo and take his chances.

Svetlana asked if she would be able to stay with the team. Bexx nodded. "Yes, of course. We'd be happy to have you remain with us."

Svetlana smiled at Special K. "Looks like I'll be in your hair a while longer, sis."

Bexx continued. "Just for the rest of you to be aware, JT told me earlier today he's made plans to leave and return home. So, when you have a moment, express to him your appreciation for his training and expertise."

# CHAPTER TWELVE

When Nick finished at *Big Jim's Eastside Tires,* he headed up the street to the local Walmart and waited at the entrance. Watching traffic, Nick was looking for a specific vehicle, one that would have current plates and registration and match his own in model make and year. No point in doing all this work to get the truck ready and then get stopped by the police. The vehicle was listed stolen, and now Nick needed new stolen plates and to dump the old ones. An hour passed, and an old farmer rolled into Walmart driving the same make and model of truck, but one year newer.

Nick mumbled, "Beggars can't be choosy, you'll do," and waited for the farmer to enter the building. Five-minutes later, the plates and registrations had been swapped, and just to be safe Nick took the old guy's insurance card as well. Nick jumped on I-94 East and headed to Washington D.C. The trip would take approximately twenty-two hours. Once in Washington D.C., Nick began to look for a public spot to meet The Director. On the long drive, he had sort of worked out a plan. Meet The Director in a public place, a park or food court, someplace that would be very public and yet allow them some privacy as well. After Nick checked into his hotel and grabbed some food, he did a Google search on his phone for local parks. There was one nearby that looked promising and within walking distance. He made a note of the directions to get to the park and then prepared to go to sleep.

The next few days would be critical, and he had to be sharp if his plan had any hope of working. Lying down, he wondered if Bexx had read the final two letters he had written yet. Looking at the ceiling, he realized there were no metal conduits to trace; the ceiling was just your basic hotel ceiling, nothing interesting to occupy his mind and lull him to sleep. He already missed the missile facility. Eventually, Nick fell asleep.

The next morning, Nick showered but did not shave. To get close to The Director, Nick had a plan, but it required blending in and appearing to be one of the many homeless in the D.C. area.

First, however, on the agenda for today was locating the perfect spot for the meeting. Nick walked out of the hotel and down Crystal Drive towards the park he had located the night before. The *Crystal City Water Park* was his destination. It was located at 1750 Crystal Drive in Arlington, Virginia, just a couple of blocks from Nick's hotel. When Nick arrived, he began a standard scout of the park, noting egress points and avenues of a possible ambush, as well as vulnerabilities from potential snipers. He had no idea what The Director would throw at him, so he wanted to be sure and set the meeting where he controlled as much of the environment as possible.

The water park was accessible by foot traffic. There was no immediate parking available, and that meant if The Director did come to the meeting, he would have to park the Black SUVs the Shāh Māt files described as his preferred mode of transportation in the D.C. area on the street. According to the files, he typically traveled light. One driver/bodyguard in a Black Tahoe with government plates. The Tahoe had been modified to accommodate his disability, so it would be easy to spot.

An hour later, Nick sat in a chair high above the modern ponds and waterfalls. He watched the people walking in the park below unaware of his presence, sitting in the private and yet immediately accessible lookout over the ponds and park. The park was perfect! Nick would be waiting in the chair as The Director arrived and guided his electric wheelchair up the seventy-five-meter ramp that gently inclined and led to the lookout point. There at the top, he would find Nick waiting at the table and chairs Nick now sat at. Nick smiled; karma was a bitch, and she appeared to like the idea of this park being the last thing The Director would ever see. Now he had to figure out how to beat the bastard at his own game. Nick stood up and began to walk back down the ramp to the park some twenty-five feet below. Time to make the final preparations and secure a chessboard.

The following morning, Nick was up early, skipped shaving again, dressed in the clothes he had purchased from a second-hand store during the short stop in Grand Forks. Checking the mirror, he smirked. He looked the part, disheveled, unshaven, wearing threadbare clothing. Time for this apparently homeless man to wash some windows. Nick left the hotel room and headed to the elevator. A woman in the hallway stepped to the side, alarmed by his sudden appearance in the hallway.

Nick stared straight ahead and mumbled, "I am the Keymaster! The Destructor is coming. Gozer the Traveler, the Destroyer," under his breath, just to increase her obvious anxiety. As they passed, he looked at her and said, "I am Vinz, Vinz Clortho, Keymaster of Gozer. Volguus Zildrohar, Lord of the Sebouillia. Are you the Gatekeeper?" She decided immediately to let him have the elevator to himself.

Perfect! Nick smiled.

The Director awoke that same morning and prepared for the day's meetings. Ian brought the custom Black Tahoe to the basement level of the parking garage and left it parked in front of the elevator doors. Pressing the only button available, the doors opened, and Ian stepped into the elevator and pressed the button for The Director's floor. Twenty-minutes later, The Director was secured in the back seat, his wheelchair stowed in the back of the storage area in the Tahoe.

Traffic was congested that morning; there was a crash on the 495 Belt route. Ian asked The Director if he would like to forgo the morning stop at the Starbucks, as was his habit. The Director thought about it for a minute. "No, Ian, let's just stick to the plan."

Ian nodded and made the necessary calls to announce The Director would be late for his meetings but would be arriving and not to cancel them. Finally, forty-five-minutes later, Ian arrived at the *North Chevy Chase Starbucks* at 8542 Connecticut Avenue and pulled the Tahoe into the parking lot.

Getting out, he asked The Director, "The usual, sir?"

"Yes, Ian, and ensure that they make it hot. Last time we were here, the drink wasn't up to standards."

"Yes, sir. Of course, sir."

Ian closed and locked the door and walked to the front door of the Starbucks.

Nick had been waiting in the parking lot, milling around, playing the part of a homeless man. Trying to blend in well enough to play the part, but not so well as to alarm the customers. One call to the local cops and his plan would go south. The Shāh Māt files had been specific. The Director liked to get his morning Green Tea Latte at this specific Starbucks on his way to the daily morning meetings. The files were very specific; the only exception to the routine was when The Director would be required to travel. Nick hadn't thought of that exception and was in near panic when The Director hadn't shown up at his usual time. Nick watched and thought, *oh shit, what if he isn't even in the country? What do I do if he's out of the country for some extended time and doesn't show up here at all?*

Nick shook his head and pushed back the anxiety. "Trust in the path," he whispered to himself. "After all this time, rebuilding the truck, finding the water park, making it here with no issues, this cannot be a coincidence. Calm down and watch. His Majesty will show up."

Nick continued milling through the garbage, pretending to look for food while watching for the modified Tahoe. Finally, it arrived, pulling in gently to the open parking lot. Parking in the middle of two parking spaces, the driver got out and spoke to the passenger in the back seat. He then closed the door, and Nick heard a chirp as the doors were locked remotely, the driver using the key fob to secure the vehicle. The time had come. Nick walked up to the Black Tahoe and tapped on the passenger door window.

The Director was sitting calmly in the back seat, reading the morning security briefing prepared by his undersecretary at the *Defense Intelligence Agency.* As he scanned the brief, he heard a tap at the window. Looking up, he saw a homeless man standing outside the Tahoe, smiling and nodding his head. The Director sighed and returned to his briefing.

Tap, tap, tap, the man knocked on the window again. "Wash your windows, sir?"

The Director did not answer. He looked for Ian and saw he was still in line, waiting for the Green Tea Latte to be prepared. The homeless man walked to the front of the Tahoe, spit on the windshield and began rubbing the mucus mixed mass of bloody snot with the sleeve on his stained and filthy olive drab field jacket.

The Director was furious. "Get the fuck away from my car, you filthy piece of shit! Do you know who the fuck I am?" he screamed from inside the vehicle. If The Director would have had the use of his legs, he would have gotten out of the vehicle and beat the homeless man bloody. However, he was unable to do much more than curse at the disgusting remnant of a human being defiling the windshield of his Tahoe.

Just when The Director thought matters couldn't get any worse, the homeless man spit another large wad of snot on the window and continued to smear the green slimy mass across the previously immaculate windshield. The Director was beside himself with fury.

Outside the Tahoe, Nick was in near ecstasy. The last time he remembered getting over on an enemy this perfectly with such a childish prank, he was a high school sophomore. He had cut class and was walking silently through the empty halls to his science teacher's classroom. Cracking the classroom door open just enough, he began pelting the science teacher, Mr. Ferguson, with one raw egg after another. The first three eggs hit Ferguson mid-torso and exploded, the fourth hit him square in the face and stunned him, and he fell to the floor, dazed. Nick had been beside himself with glee that day. Mr. Ferguson had the most offensive breath he had ever smelled and a body odor to match. Nick hated him. Mission complete, Nick left the hallway, running to the nearest garbage can and dumping the remaining raw eggs.

Nick continued smearing the windshield with his field jacket sleeve and then pulled up the windshield wiper. Quickly, he removed an envelope from the right breast pocket of the jacket and placed it under the wiper. Then he looked inside the Tahoe and smiled at the now furious Director. Nick saluted the man with a military salute modified with a final middle finger extended in a silent fuck you. Nick turned and ran, laughing at the remarkable success of his prank. The look of absolute uncontrollable rage on The Director's face was priceless. As Nick ran away, he heard The Director screaming Ian's name.

# CHAPTER THIRTEEN

Ian returned to the Tahoe carrying The Director's Green Tea Latte, unaware of Nick's antagonizing visit. When he opened the rear passenger door to hand The Director his morning pick-me-up, he knew immediately something was wrong. The Director was shaking with frustration.

"Sir, what's wrong? What happened?"

"A person, thing, a creature of some kind has spat on the windshield. It left a note under the wiper blade, Ian. Please retrieve it and then locate the nearest car wash and remove that filth from the windshield."

"Yes, sir, immediately sir, my apologies, sir! Did you see where they ran off to? Perhaps I could locate them and reprimand them."

"No, Ian. He's gone, probably crawled under the nearest rock or hiding in a filthy garbage can somewhere nearby. Just get the envelope and get the vehicle sanitized."

"Yes, sir" Ian retrieved the envelope and paused when he looked at it.

"What is it, Ian?"

"The envelope, sir. It's addressed to you."

The Director paused for a moment and considered what that meant. "Hand it to me, Ian."

"Sir, perhaps I should have Homeland Security look at it first? Who knows what the envelope contains. It could be laced with anthrax, or perhaps a nerve agent. You know the Russians aren't too happy with the latest diplomat expulsions. And your last communication with President Putin wasn't exactly friendly."

The Director smiled at the memory of his last conversation with the

Russian leader. "No, Ian, this wasn't the Russians; it was much more personal. The Russians are many things, but unprofessional isn't one. This was very unprofessional. Hand me the envelope."

"Yes, sir." Ian handed The Director the envelope and then got in the Tahoe and turned on the wipers, then the windshield wiper fluid on full, trying to remove the disgusting smears across the window.

While Ian tried to locate the nearest car wash, The Director opened the envelope carefully. Inside he found a note and a playing card, a *Hoyle* playing card. Not just any card, but the *Joker*, The Wild Card.

The Director raised an eyebrow. The Wild Card was here, right in front of him, taunting him. He put the card on the seat beside him and opened the note.

*Robert thought we should finally meet. Sorry about the windshield, but I wanted it to be memorable. Care to play a winner takes all game of chess? I understand you like the game. Meet me tomorrow at the Robert H. Smith Water Park, in Crystal City. I will be waiting for you at the top of the lookout. Be there 1100 hours.*

The Director smiled. So, The Wild Card was here in the D.C. area and challenging him to a winner takes all game of chess.

"Ian, after you clean the car, clear my calendar for tomorrow."

"The entire day, sir?"

"The entire day. I have been invited to play a game of chess. I want the day free, entirely free of distraction."

"Yes, sir."

"And Ian, I want the layout of the *Robert H. Smith Water Park* in *Crystal City* sent to my computer in half an hour."

Ian began to make the necessary arrangements as he was driving to the car wash. Fifteen-minutes later, The Director's calendar had been cleared, and the Tahoe sanitized.

Back at the missile facility, Bexx, and the team were packing. Most of what they had brought to the facility would be left behind. The armory would remain, with the exception of their original weapons. No rifles and none of the weapons Nick had purchased would be taken. Bexx wanted them to return to their roots. Diamond Dave had left early that morning. No goodbyes were spoken; he just gathered his things and walked out the door. JT would be leaving in the next morning.

While the rest of the team were gathering their belongings, Buffy and Svetlana were spending their last few moments in the Bat Cave, unsure of what exactly to do with the VSATs The Driver had purchased, specifically the military grade VSAT. The equipment was too bulky to carry, and Bexx had provided no clear direction on what she wanted them to do.

They were packing up some of the more portable equipment, cables and portable hard drives when simultaneously across all the computer screens an email message popped up. It appeared in every email account they had open, and every message window. Simultaneously, a message appeared on the VSAT terminal screens, including the military-grade VSAT. The message was short and specific.

*The Wild Card has set a chess match with Robert Taylor. I need to speak to Tamriko now, waiting.*

Svetlana and Buffy checked the messages and saw they were all the same and contained the exact same content. They looked at each other, eyebrows raised.

"What the hell does this mean?" Buffy finally said.

Svetlana answered, "I have no idea."

Buffy paused for a minute and then said, "Don't change anything. I'm going to get Bexx."

A short time later, Buffy returned to the Bat Cave with Bexx and showed her the message. The same message, across every account and even on the VSATs. They took her to the roof and showed her the military grade VSAT as well. Bexx was silent for several moments, analyzing the meaning of using her real name, Nick's nickname in The Director's world and the wish to communicate immediately. After several moments, she took a deep breath.

Turning to Buffy, she asked, "Which system would be the most secure to communicate on?"

Buffy nodded to the military grade VSAT and said, "That one, but also it seems the riskiest. We have no idea who is messaging or what their intentions are."

Bexx nodded. "Understood."

Bexx sat down at the terminal and began to type.

*I am here, who are you?*

Seconds later, there was a response. *Verify this is Tamriko?*

*It is, who are you? What do you want?*

*I am a friend; I sent you the Shāh Māt files.*

Bexx paused. Nick had said there was something weird about the files; they contained too much information. Details that had nothing to do with any security clearance needs. Someone had compiled the information and then removed it after they had accessed it. Nick had asked Buffy to check, and when she had, the files were gone.

Bexx replied, *Friend, how do I know what you say is true, and how do you know me?*

*I knew your father. We worked together.*

Bexx was shaken at the mention of her father but recovered immediately. Whomever it was, was trying to manipulate her.

*Okay friend tell me how you knew my father and me. Something no one else would know, or we are done here.* Bexx pushed send and waited.

*Are we alone?* Was the reply.

*No, I am here with friends.*

*We need to be alone to continue.*

Bexx stared at the screen. Once more into Nick's dark world of conspiracy and double crosses.

She finally spoke to Svetlana and Buffy. "Leave us. If I need you, I'll call for you. Continue the preparations for our move."

Buffy and Svetlana turned and walked towards the rooftop ladder. Bexx waited until they were gone.

*I am alone.*

*When you were a child, very young, perhaps two or three, you were driving with your father in the country. You were in the back seat of the car. You asked him if he could hear you and then went silent and bobbed your head back and forth. He watched you in the rear-view mirror and said no, tiny, I can't hear you, tiny was his nickname for you. You asked him to listen again, and again silence as your head bobbed back and forth. Again, he said, No, I can't hear you. What are you doing? You replied I am singing in my head, Papa. Listen again. Your father smiled when he told me this story.*

Bexx sat motionless reading the text, tears streaming down her face. It took her a moment to gain control over her emotions.

Finally, she typed, *what song was I singing?*

*Butterfly, Butterfly, happy all day,* was the response.

Bexx was unable to respond for several minutes as she cried reliving the childhood memory of singing to her father silently from the back of the car.

Finally, she responded, *what do you want?*

*I have a proposal for you. The Wild Card has set up a meeting with Director Taylor for tomorrow morning, at 1100 hours. Assuming he is following his past patterns, this will be a fatal confrontation for one or both of them. I may be able to even the odds of his survival. I will be able to provide you with a live feed of their meeting if you are interested.*

Bexx thought for a moment. A proposal meant something in exchange for this offer of assistance.

*And your proposal is exactly what?*

*I provide you proof that I can do what I say I can do. I can't take Director Taylor down myself, but at the right moment, I can even the odds. If I do that and show you proof I have done it, will you consider working for me, you and your team?*

*I'll consider it. How will I watch the live feed?*

*I'll send it here, on the VSAT, starting tomorrow at 1000 hours. Watch it alone.*

*Why alone?*

*Trust no one. Not everyone on your team is who they appear to be. Be here at 1000 hours tomorrow.*

*Understood. One last question, have we met?*

The VSAT terminal went quiet.

# CHAPTER FOURTEEN

Nick sat alone in the dark of his hotel room. In twenty-four hours, it would be over, one way or the other it would be finished. Either he would win, The Director would win, or they would both be dead. Two out of three wasn't bad odds. Nick stared at the wall and wondered what Bexx was doing. Probably pacing back and forth in the missile facility, cursing him for taking off on his own. That was the best-case scenario in his head. Worst-case scenario? She was gone, the team was gone. The place was empty, the sounds of life removed from the former cold war relic. He tried not to consider that option. Winning one of the two options in the deathmatch with The Director was all that mattered now.

The Director was sitting in his wheelchair, Ian always present to care for his needs. The Director reviewed the plan for the water park meeting the next day. A security detail would be present just in case The Wild Card had some sneaky shit up his sleeve. Seemed to be his forte, pulling a rabbit out of a hat that appeared to be completely empty. Had they met under other circumstances, his quirky skill set would have been an invaluable asset. As it was now, he was a tremendous pain in The Director's ass. The Director smiled at that thought. Payback was a bitch, and Nick, The Wild Card, was about to experience payback as only The Director could deliver.

In the back of his mind, The Director heard Ian clear his throat and then sigh. The Director paused. "Yes, Ian, that's the third time you've sighed in the past twenty-minutes. Out with it."

Ian quietly replied. "Sir, I know you covered every detail and contingency; however, I'm concerned about you being so close to someone so…unpredictable. It is a risk, sir, a risk I can see no real benefit in embracing."

The Director paused, rubbing his eyes. "Yes, I understand there is a risk, but what I have planned makes this risk cost-effective, Ian. The idea of seeing The Wild Card face to face when I defeat him at his own game, watching as my security detail secures him in one of the Tahoe's. Knowing the next few days he lives will be his last and filled with pain beyond measure. That is the reward. The risk will be minimal, the reward great. It is a basic cost-benefit analysis, Ian, and the potential cost will be minimized by good contingency planning. For example, you know about the hacker I have embedded in The Wild Card's little freak show. He's been feeding me information since Camp Baroota fell. And you know about the sniper who's also embedded. What you don't know is, the hacker helped me turn one member of the dyke freak show to our side, and then she turned another. Two of them working for me! In addition to the hacker and the sniper." The Director laughed out loud. "Hell, in a few more months I could have turned the entire team against him. He would be alone in that damn fortress of a missile facility. That would have been ideal, to see him crushed by his own team. But then he showed up here, and my timeline had to be accelerated."

"Yes, sir, that's exactly what concerns me. Now you're on his timeline." Ian spoke quietly but firmly.

The Director nodded, thinking quietly. "Yes, however, Ian, my sources tell me he's entirely alone in this endeavor. He left North Dakota with no plan in mind. This is a suicide run, Ian. He has no intention of returning, and it gets better."

"How so, sir?" Ian asked, puzzled.

"My sources tell me the woman he was with has ended their relationship. She leads the team, and the team is packing as we speak, preparing to leave at her direction. Soon, the facility will be mine once again. The Wild Card will be out of my world, and the team that is now vacating the facility will be working for me in whatever manner I decide."

Ian stared at the floor, quiet for another moment, thinking.

"Out with it, Ian! Speak your mind."

Ian cleared his throat. "Sir, a man who has nothing to lose, no reason to hesitate. That is the most dangerous opponent you can possibly face."

The Director nodded. "Exactly, and given his past pattern of unpredictability, he is even more dangerous. Precisely why I'm planning this operation personally. Seeing that every eventuality is addressed."

Ian closed his eyes. The Director's mind was made up. He was much too close to this particular problem to see it clearly. Ian knew he could not change The Director's mind. He took in a deep breath and exhaled. "Yes, sir. As you wish, sir," he said with some apprehension.

Bexx sat outside the facility, in the dark, on the edge of a concrete lid to one of the twelve silos. The team was packed and ready, waiting for her to give the word to leave. Bexx was conflicted. Should she watch the meeting with Nick and The Director at all? Perhaps the best plan was to move on, take the deal offered by the VSAT mystery sponsor regardless of if Nick received help or not. She was tired, deep down tired. The kind of tired where you just don't give a damn about anything anymore. The life Nick lived was exciting but ultimately exhausting. At least in Ukraine, the enemy was understood, tangible and clearly defined. Since she entered Nick's twisted life, the enemy could be everyone and anyone. Now she had two members of her own team turned against her. This world was toxic, for every one of them, nothing but poison. She had to leave to save the team, to save herself. Nick was radioactive, and his vision was destroying them, all of them.

Finally, she stood up. Her mind was made up; she would watch. Either Nick would die horribly, or The Director would, or perhaps both. Either way, she needed to know. Would their enemy survive, or would her former lover perish?

In the basement of an unmarked government building a mere couple of miles from The Director's apartment, the shadowy silent figure sat quietly in the office chair. The risk about to be taken was enormous. To take sides against Director Taylor was a tactical nightmare. The man had never been defeated. Years of surviving the internal government back-stabbing at the highest levels of power had sharpened what had already been a formidable second sight. Director Taylor had an uncanny ability to sniff out a trap, particularly a lethal trap, and turn the circumstances around to his own favor. He'd survived multiple assassination attempts, from both foreign interests and powers within his own government. The man could not be killed. The collection of proverbial skeletons he'd collected and housed in his own dark but useful closets had enabled him to pull the true levers of power in Washington for decades. The time had come to try once again to return the balance.

The Wild Card had shown an unusual skill set The Director had never been able to gain an understanding of. A psychological profile of The Wild Card had been conducted in secret, and the results were enlightening. The two men were remarkably similar. Damaged as children, surrounded by abusive parents and authority figures during childhood, they somehow survived. Each was single-minded in their focus and pursuits. And each had a nearly unexplainable ability to survive, anticipate their opponent and turn a deadly disadvantage to an advantage.

The Wild Card had set up a chess game with Director Taylor. The Shadowy figure smiled; an excellent method to draw The Director out into the open. He'd never been defeated at chess, and The Wild Card understood this. They had been engaged in a life and death chess match for months in the real world, and now it was time for a final confrontation on a real chessboard. Given The Director had an obvious sense of invincibility in the game, he wouldn't refuse. The Wild Card must have known that. Planned for it. The time to act was now. Time to push all the chips on the table into the pot and make the final move.

The Shadowy figure requested an electronic surveillance of the meeting separate from Director Taylor's men. Additionally, a coded order was issued, and The Director's security detail communication frequencies would be accessed. If the moment arose, the security detail's Comms would be hacked, and an order given. The security team would comply; they had no choice given the severity of the order. Their years of training demanded absolute compliance with this order. Under no circumstances would they ever question it. It was ingrained in their training and tested time and time again. Psychologically, it was considered a conditioned response. When Pavlov rang this proverbial bell, the security dogs would have no choice but to comply.

# CHAPTER FIFTEEN

Nick finally fell asleep sometime that night. How long he'd been sleeping, he had no idea. The alarm went off, and he ejected himself from the hotel bed, disoriented. It took a moment to re-member where he was, and then the reality of today's meeting hit him. Time to prepare. Nick picked up the report he'd been reading from the Shāh Māt files the night before; it was the earliest account of Director Taylor's life in the file. It hit him way too close to home.

*Kris Taylor was a single mom, raising two small boys and work-ing minimum wage jobs. She had a problem with addiction. Addiction to drugs, alcohol, sex, and addiction to pornography. Her issues with addiction created a situation the boy's father couldn't tolerate, so he left them. The boys moved from a duplex to a two-bed hotel room, sharing one bed while their mother shared the other with whomever she brought home from her job at a nearby bar. The oldest boy, Troy, remembered waking up often to the sounds of his mother and the latest man she had found rutting away in the bed next to theirs. This was a nightly occur-rence according to Troy. Robert had no memory of the events in the hotel room.*

*After about a year, they moved into another duplex. Here, Robert's memories begin to take shape. Being an addict to sex, as well as pornog-raphy, Kris kept various sex toys all over the house, constantly ready for use. The boys grew up with vibrators plugged in next to their recharge-able toothbrushes. Gels for oral and anal sex were on the bathroom countertop next to their toothpaste. This was their normal. Kris believed this gave them a healthier outlook on sex and masturbation. The boys at the time were four years old and one and a half years old. One of youngest boy's first defining events was waking up hungry one day and stumbling into the kitchen to find some food. He found a large dill pickle in the fridge and took it for his own. Walking to the sliding glass door, he saw the kids were out at recess in the school behind their duplex. They were bigger kids, elementary school age, and he wanted to play with them. He opened the door and stumbled out of the house in diapers to the fence that separated their yard from the school playground. He sat and watched at the fence, waving and smiling as he ate his pickle. Sever-*

*al of the girls came over to the fence and tried to talk to him. He smiled and tried to talk to them.*

*Robert smelled terrible; he was covered in dirt and grime, as his mother rarely bathed him, and he was late on his toilet training. He wore a diaper that sagged from the weight of its considerable contents. Shit had run down his legs and dried. The girls were a little bit horrified at the smell as he tried to greet them. Meanwhile, Kris had woken up and went to the fridge; discovering the pickle was gone, she looked for the boys. She saw her youngest boy at the fence, waving the pickle around as he talked to the girls, and walked outside, irritated and still hungover from the previous night's party. Kris was angry her son had taken her favorite sex toy of the moment and perhaps a little bit jealous of her son and the attention he was getting from the small group of little girls maybe 7 or 8 years old. So, she walked up said, "HI girls" and then chastised her youngest son for taking Mommy's favorite dildo from the fridge. She said to the girls, "He just won't leave my sex toys alone. He loves the taste of the pickle after I use it. Someday, perhaps one of you will benefit from that acquired taste?" Kris smiled an evil smile and pulled the boy back to the house. Most of the girls had some idea of what she had said and immediately replied with the typical "Ewww gross" girls of that age respond with and ran off.*

*Their nickname for the boy, the one eating the pickle, had been set in stone. Word traveled around the elementary school, and the next day when he went outside, there were boys and a couple of girls waiting. Robert was happy and ran to the fence to meet his new friends. The boys spit on him and called him a pickle eating queer. One boy dropped his pants and peed through the fence all over Robert while the other kids watched and laughed. "Pickle" was born. The nickname would stick until Robert himself was in school and savagely beat anyone who dared speak the nickname to him. That didn't prevent the name from being spoken in private, dark conversations all through the school. Even the teachers became aware of the story and laughed about it in the faculty room.*

*"Pickle" followed Robert for all of his childhood according to his older brother, Troy Taylor. He is the source for this story. He remarked the nickname followed Robert through school until he left for college.*

*According to Troy, this moment framed Robert's early childhood more than any other event.*

Nick stared darkly out the window, instantly immersed in his own nightmare of a childhood. It made sense; of course, they had common threads of abuse, shame and dark moments that framed their rage. He could use this to his advantage. He smiled and dressed, then grabbed the bag of assorted items he'd purchased during the trip from the missile facility to the Washington, D.C. area. Random miscellaneous items, all lethal and none of which he planned to use. They were a distraction from the real plan. The purpose of these weapons was to provide The Director with a false sense of security. Once they were discovered and removed from the area around the water park, The Director would hopefully relax a bit, confident his intricate planning had defeated Nick's.

Nick left the hotel room and headed towards the elevator. No one spoke to him. His appearance had degraded further in the past forty-eight hours, no shower or shave this morning, although he'd brushed his teeth. Now was not the time to drop the façade of being desperate and broken. The elevator ride to the lobby floor seemed nearly instantaneous, and the doors opened much sooner than he expected. Nick stepped out into the lobby and walked to the hotel's front doors. The clerk behind the desk smiled mechanically and then seeing Nick's appearance, his smile wavered.

"Have a good day, sir," he announced less as a greeting and more in a tone that suggested he hoped Nick would not be returning to the hotel anytime soon.

Nick nodded and mumbled, "You too," then stepped out onto the street and began the short mile walk from the hotel to the water park.

Once at the water park, Nick stopped and checked the people who'd already arrived there. He planned on The Director having his people already present and watching everything he did. They were already here, he had no doubt, hiding in plain sight. Pretending to be regular patrons of the park. Nick had spent every minute possible in the park, trying to gain an understanding of what was a typical day and who frequented the park on a regular basis. Hoping to understand a break in the healthy flow of the park. The park felt alien today. Something was off, but he couldn't quite figure out what it was. Nick rechecked the park. Nothing.

"Hmm," he mumbled. "Perhaps today will be more challenging than I originally thought. I know you're out there, but I can't see you...not yet."

Nick taped a knife under the table where they would play chess, a set of wire cutters under the chair The Director would have to move to pull his wheelchair up to the table. Random items meant to be found. Ice pick here, corkscrew there. All weapons and all ordinary items able to be acquired in any department or hardware store. Nick planned on being physically searched by The Director's security detail before he would actually arrive. So, he'd hidden items in his clothing as well. A finger saw and boxcutter blades were hidden in his ball cap, a belt buckle knife hidden in plain sight on a new belt. Once everything had been placed in plain sight, Nick pulled out a leather covered metal flask and opened it. Taking a small sip, just enough to make his breath smell like alcohol, he replaced the cap. Then he took out a pack of Marlboro cigarettes and a green Bic lighter and lit up. Inhaling deeply, Nick took a drag on the cigarette, paused, then exhaled. It was now one hour before the game was scheduled to begin.

The Director was sitting in his office, watching the live video feeds of Nick's pathetic attempts to place weapons around the park. He smiled; Nick's juvenile planning would be no match for his meticulous preparations. The park would be secured and sanitized, and all weapons removed long before he would even consider entering the chess match. Finally, Nick sat down at the table and took a quick nip from a flask he kept in the front pocket of his vintage field jacket. The Director chuckled deeply. The one swallow of alcohol told him everything he needed to know. Nick was nowhere near as prepared and composed as he was trying to display. And now he was smoking too? A new habit? The information he'd received via his spies on the team had been accurate. Nick was coming apart at the seams. Perfect. Let him have his little vices.

A message came in from the observation team already set up in the park. Should they remove the items Nick had deposited? The Director told them to hold off until he was en route. Let Nick have a little bit of confidence now and then pull the rug out from under him. This way was preferred; the effect of having some hope and then having it removed would be more disturbing. Nick had no idea the chess match had already begun.

Ian watched the live feeds as well. He didn't like the way Nick had so casually placed the items in the park; it felt wrong. He'd read the reports about how Nick had dismantled both Baroota and Cachibaché. He intuitively found a weakness and exploited it. This seemed much too easy, too orchestrated, He wanted to suggest to Director Taylor just to take Nick by force and not play the game of chess, but instead, he said nothing. Ian already knew The Director had made up his mind.

While The Director watched the live feed from the area security cameras and began to make his preparations to depart for the water park, Bexx had taken a seat in front of the military grade VSAT and logged on. A few moments later, a message popped up.

*Good morning. We'll have live video and audio feeds for today's chess game. How did you sleep?*

*I slept. I'm curious, how will you achieve live audio? I assume the video will be from camera feeds in the park or a drone perhaps. But live audio seems like a stretch.*

*I have a secret. As you know, The Director is confined to a wheel-chair. The last maintenance cycle performed on the chair came with an additional upgrade. I had the chair fitted with an audio surveillance device.*

*I see, makes sense. Before we begin, I have one additional request. If my team and I are to begin working for you, it will be without Nick. If he survives today's game, he is not a part of the agreement. Understood?*

There was a long pause, several minutes before an answer came.

*Are you sure? He brings an element to the team that can't be trained or planned for. Your team is much more successful when he's involved.*

*This is non-negotiable. Nick is out. The team is more functional without his influence.*

*Are you sure you wish to continue, then? I can withdraw my assistance should the opportunity ever present itself. There are no guarantees I'll be able to do anything. We may just sit here and watch him die.*

*Understood. No, I'll remain and watch the match. Let's proceed.*

*Before we proceed, I need to know you're alone. Should Director Taylor survive, I can't afford to have one of his spies feeding him the information I've already told you. I'm taking a huge risk by coming out of the shadows and attempting to influence the outcome of this match. The only reason I've made this offer is your Wild Card and his unprecedented success in defeating The Director and his men. Are we clear? Not one of your team can be present during this live feed. If Director Taylor wins, we'll have to find a way to remove his spies from your team before you'll be employed. Agreed?*

Bexx thought for a minute, then finally answered, *Agreed. I am alone.*

The video feed began. Bexx could see Nick sitting in a plastic chair at the top of a path that overlooked the water park. He had just sat down and pulled out a container of some kind from the front pocket of his jacket. He took a drink from the container and then secure the lid. A look of surprise came across her face when Nick lit a cigarette, inhaled and blew out a puff of smoke. Bexx thought silently, Nick doesn't smoke, or at least he didn't while we were together.

*Can you zoom in on Nick?* she typed.

*The Director is leaving now and will be en route. The trip will take approximately twenty-minutes before he reaches the water park. I will activate the audio surveillance when he arrives.*

*Understood.*

After a pause, the camera zoomed in. Nick looked disheveled, his hair barely combed, and several days' growth of a salt and pepper beard had appeared on his face. He always shaved when they'd been together. Honestly, he looked like shit. Bexx was worried; perhaps their breakup and the road trip had been harder on Nick than she'd realized.

She mumbled under her breath, "Now is not the time to fall apart. This guy will eat your lunch. Gear up! He's coming." Bexx sat back quietly, but she could feel her heartbeat and breathe gently increase. She took a deep breath and waited.

# CHAPTER SIXTEEN

Nick watched the park, waiting for some sign The Director's people had arrived. At thirty-minutes to the hour, thirty-minutes until their game was supposed to begin, a couple who had been lounging in the grass on a blanket got up. They'd been laughing and joking, making quiet, intimate conversation. Now they were all business, the façade had dropped. The man gathered the blanket and two bottles of water they'd been drinking and put them in the backpack they'd brought. The woman began collecting a few of the weapons Nick had placed randomly throughout the park. Nick smiled as he watched another guy who had been reading a book and sitting by one of the fountains close the book. He got up and tossed the book in the closest garbage can and then also began to collect the items Nick had left. Nick placed both hands on the table in plain sight and waited; The Director was apparently on his way. Nick picked up the flask of vodka and took another sip. There were two other people who watched Nick; they didn't move. Their sole job was to ensure that no matter what happened, he didn't escape. Once he arrived, he wouldn't be allowed to leave. The Director had been waiting to get Nick in a place that would end his disruptive run for some time. He didn't plan on letting this opportunity slip away.

Ian informed The Director the preparations to secure and sanitize the water park had begun. The Director nodded. "Excellent, Ian. I'll be ready to depart in ten-minutes. Ensure the extra security detail is here waiting when we're ready to depart. I want them to arrive with us, in convoy fashion, to make an impression on this Philistine."

"Yes, sir, and if I may, sir, I would like to personally search your opponent. I don't want to leave anything to chance. Would that be an option, sir?"

Ian hesitated. The Director noticed he was conflicted and waited, watching his facial muscles tighten.

"What is it, Ian? Out with it!"

"Sir, you pay me to protect you, you pay me for my insight and perhaps my intuition. I think you should consider taking extra and extraordinary precaution for this event."

"What do you suggest, Ian?"

"I have a very bad feeling about this Wild Card, sir. Something about him isn't right. His methods are too…erratic and unpredictable. I think you should cancel the game. Please consider it, sir."

Director Taylor smiled. "Of course, I'll consider it, Ian, I appreciate the personal touch you're lending to my safety."

"My pleasure, sir."

Ten-minutes later, the security detail arrived. Ian escorted The Director to his custom Tahoe, and they left as a group, with The Director's Tahoe in the second position of a total of four Tahoes driving as one unit.

"Ian, when we arrive, I would like the security detail to fan out and take up positions within the park. When they are set up, I would like two of them to proceed up the ramp to where our little game is to occur. They will need to search the area and The Wild Card's possessions. When they've completed that task and the all clear is given, you and I will exit the vehicle and you may accompany me to the table. Did you bring my custom chess set?"

"Yes, sir. It's here, in the vehicle."

"Excellent. I want to leave nothing to chance. No point in searching him and then finding out he poisoned my chess pieces. If he has a chessboard, it will be removed."

"Understood, sir."

"When you've completed searching him and removed any potential threats, I'll want my own chessboard set up; white pieces set up on his side. He will begin the match. Best to let him think he has some advantage."

"Yes, sir."

Nick heard the Tahoe caravan coming long before it arrived. The lead Tahoe cleared traffic with a short blast from a police siren, and subdued flashing red and blue lights in the grill did the rest. The Director arrived with a purpose and a message. People who had been legitimately enjoying the water park's peaceful water fountains and green lawns began to leave. Whatever this was, they wanted no part of it. Nick began setting up the cheap chess set he'd purchased at Walmart the day before. The security detail exited the vehicles and began a second sweep of the park, looking for any possible threat to their charge. Nick took a deep breath and waited. Finally, three men approached him specifically. They weren't your typical undercover government types. They wore tactical gear and made no pretenses about their purpose.

The lead agent said, "Stand up, please, and keep your hands where we can see them."

Nick nodded and held his hands at shoulder level and stood slowly and smiled.

"What's up, fellas? Expecting some kind of *Jason Bourne* shit from an old man wanting to play a simple game of chess?"

The lead agent stepped forward and asked, "Do you have any weapons? Anything that could cause me harm?"

"Nope, Just a flask of vodka, a pack of *Marlboro Reds* and a *Bic* lighter."

The agent began his search of Nick and his clothing. They took off his hat and placed it on the table and then began a typical government style weapons search. Law enforcement has a very different pattern and type of searching method than government trained officers. Nick knew by this action, the agents' training and experience would be very different than his own.

When the search was done, the agent picked up the ball cap and turned it inside out. Two single-edged razor blades and a wire finger saw fell out.

"What the fuck is this?" the agent asked, suddenly alarmed. "You said you had nothing, no weapons!"

Nick shrugged. "I like to carve wood. You never know when you find a tree limb that brings on the urge."

The lead agent wasn't amused and punched Nick in the upper abdomen. "Any other hobbies you want to confess to, asshole?"

Nick doubled over, unable to respond immediately. Finally, he shook his head and managed to whisper, "No."

"You'd better hope so," the agent snarled and continued examining the ball cap. When he was done, he told Nick to remove his boots and belt.

Nick removed the belt and placed it on the table. One of the agents picked it up and examined the belt buckle. He nodded to the lead agent as he removed a small knife concealed as part of the buckle.

Nick shrugged and smiled sheepishly. "Sorry, forgot about that one."

They then examined his boots. Two more knives were located and removed. The lead agent punched Nick again and then grabbed his jacket, pulling him back upright.

His face within inches of Nick's, he growled, "When this bull-shit is over, you're mine. We have a long drive back to the holding area you'll be going to. You'll regret this."

Nick nodded. "Thanks for the heads up. Do you speak to all your dates this way? Into the rough stuff, I see. One of those *Christian Grey* types, all handcuffs and nipple clips. It's all fun and games until the cray ex-girlfriend shows up and starts stabbing the kid's rabbit."

The lead agent shoved Nick into the chair and turned to his shoulder mic. Keying the mic, he said, "He's clear. The Director may proceed."

From the VSAT terminal, Bexx watched as the contact with Nick was made. It appeared to be relatively peaceful until the lead agent punched Nick the first time. She sighed and shook her head. "Of course. You're a thousand miles from help, outnumbered and outgunned, and can't stop being you."

The second punch looked worse. Nick doubled over, and then the agent pulled him back upright and came face to face.

Bexx lowered her head and thought, *I hope you have some kind of plan, or this is going to be very ugly.*

Ian was waiting in the second Tahoe for confirmation the park and Nick had been searched and secured. He watched as Nick received the attitude correction from the lead agent.

"Sir, I believe the lead agent is making it clear this will be a very memorable day for your opponent."

"Yes, Ian. I'm watching. Make sure to get the man's name. He may be useful in future operations."

"Yes, sir."

When the lead agent announced over the radio that the scene was now secure and The Director would be safe exiting the vehicle, Ian replied, "Remove the chessboard as well." When the board was secured, Ian looked in the rearview mirror and said, "Sir, they're ready. What are your orders?"

There was a brief pause, and then a man exited the vehicle and began to walk up the wheelchair accessible ramp towards Nick. Ian passed the agents walking back down the ramp carrying the weapons they'd taken off Nick. He heard the lead agent muttering, "That piece of shit will hate the day I was born before this day is over." Ian wondered what Nick had said to get under the man's skin so quickly. As he approached, Nick stood up and smiled.

Nick reached out his hand to shake Ian's; Ian refused.

Nick shrugged. "What's next? A little waterboarding? Drill a tooth or two? Remove a couple of my fingernails?"

Ian said, "An additional search, just to be sure there was nothing missed."

"Works for me." Nick raised his arms. "Your predecessor is a lefty, so if you could take your cheap shots from the right, I'd appreciate it. Pretty sure he at least cracked one of my ribs."

Ian said, "Just an additional search to make sure nothing was missed, and then I'll set up The Director's custom chessboard."

"Understood." Nick kept his hands up at shoulder level.

Ian said, "Turn, please, and place your hands behind your head, interlace your fingers." Nick complied. "Spread your legs." Nick spread his legs shoulder-width apart.

Ian stepped in and simultaneously grabbed the hands interlaced on Nick's head.

*Another government puke,* Nick thought, *same old shit, no imagination, Jesus, these guys are predictable. Trained like robots. Rule following pussies. Wonder what his psych eval looks like?*

"So what's your name, and what is it you do for Director Taylor?"

"Ian, and I'm his personal assistant and driver. Why do you want to know my name?" Ian responded.

"Oh, lucky you. Personal assistant, huh? So tell me, do you wipe his ass with adult wipes or baby wipes after he shits the Depends? And the name? Ian? All his drivers have the same damn name. What does that say about you?"

Ian stiffened. "I don't like your tone, sir."

"Sorry, Ian, just curious. Last night as I was sitting in bed watching Ironside reruns, it occurred to me: How does a guy in a wheelchair wipe his ass? Then it came to me, his assistant does! Duh! Of course. Then I wondered, adult or baby wipes? I'm guessing a manly man like Director Taylor would use adult wipes, probably scented with *Old Spice.* Can't have people getting the wrong idea and thinking he has a soft spot. The second thought I had? Who the hell wants that job? Applies for that job? Interviews for that job? And now I know, you do! The resume you must have! Tactical ass wiping specialist! Well, at least there's the driving part to make it seem legit. By the way, get the windshield cleaned off?"

Ian continued his search, trying to focus on the task at hand. When he completed the search, he released Nick and glared at him for a moment. "Good luck today, sir. I believe you'll need it."

"Thanks, Ian, and don't forget the adult diaper bag on your way back up here. You never know when the next call of duty will arise." Nick made his standard "Fuck you" middle finger military salute, then sat down, opened the flask and took another drink.

Ian returned to the Tahoe and prepared the wheelchair for Director Taylor's exit. He opened the door and helped Director Taylor into the chair.

"Well, Ian, how was he?"

Ian cleared his throat, his face still red from the encounter with Nick. "Kick his ass, sir," was his final reply.

"Of course, Ian. Of course."

# CHAPTER SEVENTEEN

T he VSAT terminal suddenly had an audio feed as the wheelchair was removed from the back of the Tahoe. Bexx heard the exchange between The Director and Ian and rubbed her forehead. She could hear the motor on The Director's electric wheelchair as he made his way towards the ramp. On the video feed, she saw two of the security detail fall in behind him, walking at a discrete distance. Ian was at his side.

Bexx typed on the VSAT terminal's keyboard.

*And what is it exactly you'll be able to do to even these odds? Nick is outnumbered thirteen to one, and that's just the tactical guys. Who knows how many others there are hidden in the mix.*

*I can even the odds.* Will you consider now agreeing to my proposal?

*I'll wait to see the result,* Bexx replied.

She continued to watch and listen to the hmm of the wheelchair's motor as it labored, carrying The Director up the gradual incline of the ramp.

As The Director approached, Nick took a deep breath. So far, good to go. The chess game has already begun, and I still have my ace in the hole. Now to mind fuck this asshole until he can barely contain his rage and that too will be a distraction. Unfortunately, he brought the security detail, which will make killing his ass more difficult, but still possible.

Nick stood up as The Director approached.

"Good morning, Robert. I had a chessboard all ready, but the testosterone-laden crew you sent seemed to think it was a threat. A bit paranoid, aren't they?"

The Director smiled in return. "You don't get to my station in life by leaving things to chance, Nick. Attention to detail is a must. I've brought my own chessboard."

Nick nodded. "Guess that's why I never attained your station, Robert. I like to wing it, play it by ear; spontaneity is the key to an exciting life."

Ian stepped forward and produced the custom hand carved chessboard. He placed the pieces on the board one at a time, carefully.

Nick raised his eyebrows. "Giving me the white pieces, I see. Thank you, Robert! Or is it that you're so confident you'll win the match, you're giving me the first move?"

"Just being courteous."

"Ahh, I see. Well, since we're being courteous, let's at least be gentlemen about this." Nick reached out his hand. "Nick Hudson, sir."

The Director paused. Looking at Nick and then his hand, he finally reached out his own hand and replied, "Director Robert Taylor." As they shook hands, eyes locked, neither man released his grip or looked away. For a moment, Nick saw something flicker in The Director's eyes.

Nick smiled. "Good to finally meet you, sir."

The Director smiled slightly; even here, The Wild Card referred to him as sir. He was already defeated and had no clue. It was in his blood, his DNA, in fact, to subordinate to people of power. He'd been conditioned from the time he was a small child to follow. Now, here, playing the game of his life with his most formidable enemy, he couldn't help acknowledging his betters.

Nick smiled slightly, took another swig from the flask and said, "Shall we begin, sir?"

"Yes," said The Director.

A thousand miles away, watching on the VSAT, Bexx listened and wondered what the hell was up Nick's sleeve. Calling The Director sir? And he continued to drink from the flask. How did he expect to win the game if he was three sheets to the wind before it was even started?

Nick began the game with a traditional "Bird's Opening," moving the king's bishop's pawn two places forward. It left his kingside vulnerable too but offered an excellent attacking position.

Nick sat back and waited for The Director's first move.

The Director decided to mirror Nick's move for the moment and placed his pawn directly in front of the newly moved pawn. Nick immediately responded with a modified "King's Gambit." Instead of responding with his bishop, he moved his king's side knight.

Nick sat back and watched The Director. He was engrossed in the game already. The King's Gambit was an aggressive move. A modified gambit wasn't tradition by any means. Now was the time to begin the real chess match.

"Would you like a pickle, sir?"

The Director immediately looked up, his heart beating rapidly. "What did you say?" He could barely contain his anger.

Nick smiled and said, "You're in a bit of a pickle already, aren't you, sir?

The Director's eyes narrowed. "No, not yet. I see you started with 'Bird's Opening', followed by using the modified 'King's Gambit'. Nicely played."

Nick replied, "Huh? What? Bird Gambit? King's Opening? What the hell are those? Is that chess slang for 'I'm kicking your ass already'?"

The Director's face was red. "You've never heard of either move?"

"No, sir. I learned to play in the military. Sitting in a hardened facility, guarding nukes. We played for hours. No one knew how or studied the game. I just played. I don't have any formal training in it."

At the VSAT, Bexx received a typed message. *Is that true, what Nick just told Director Taylor? He has no formal chess playing education?*

She replied, *Yes, as far as I know. But if you know Nick, you understand it isn't wise to underestimate him in anything.*

The reply came back, *Then why did he choose chess? The Director is a Master. Few know this, but he's ranked in the in the FIDE as a Master. In the USCF, he's ranked as a Senior Master. Nick has no chance of winning this game.*

Bexx didn't reply.

Nick waited patiently and then finally spoke. "Robert, while you fumble fuck around trying to figure out your next move, do you mind if I look at the mechanics of your wheelchair? I'm a bit of a shade tree mechanic. I love seeing how engineers solve the problems they encounter while designing a piece of machinery like your chair. You can have your eunuch warriors, *The Unsullied*, keep an eye on me. Promise no crazy stuff, just checking out the chair, and Ian is here as well with adult wipes at the ready just in case. What do you say?" Nick stood up.

The tactical team stepped forward as soon as Nick stood up.

"Easy, boys," Nick replied, smiling. "Being a eunuch has its advantages, I guess. Focused on the task at hand and not the chicks walking past on the sidewalk. No wonder *Daenerys* and The Director trusts you so much."

The Director was at a loss; he had no idea what Nick was referring to. Something about eunuchs and his wheelchair. And what was that about adult wipes?

"Ian," The Director said over his shoulder.

"Yes, sir, I'm here."

Director Taylor turned to Nick and said, "Why not? You may look at the chair. It's custom made."

Nick smiled and said, "I bet. Probably a *Cyberdyne T-1000* model. Top tier chair, I'm told."

Nick walked carefully around the table, hands up, smiling at the two members of the tactical team. "Easy, homies. Just because I still got my junk, no need to get all envious on me."

Nick knelt at the rear of the chair and began talking. "Nope, not *Cyberdyne.* It's a *Weyland Corporation* chair. Model *LV 426.* Wow! Sir, this is top tier."

Nick moved around, touching the various electronic parts, and shifted to his right, blocking Ian's view just for a moment. At the same time, he engaged the manual right rear wheel lock. The Director was now stuck.

Nick smiled as he got up and placed a hand on The Director's right shoulder. "Excellent choice, sir. *Weyland* is the *Cadillac* of wheelchairs. Watch out for the face huggers, though."

Nothing Nick said made sense to Ian or the tactical team. *The Unsullied,* face huggers, and the *T-1000* sounded vaguely familiar to Ian, but he couldn't remember where he'd heard it before.

Nick sat back down and waited patiently for The Director's next move. The Director decided to run with the classic defense to the "King's Gambit" and brought his king's bishop to mid-board. Nick studied the board briefly and moved his king's side knight to just behind the now stronghold of white pawns in the middle of the board. He leaned back and smiled.

"Robert, while you stratificate your next move, can I ask you a question that's been bothering me for some time?"

The Director did not look up but said, "Strategize? You mean strategize?"

"Yeah, strategize, that's right. Watched too many George W. Bush press conferences, I guess."

The Director looked at Nick and rubbed his forehead. "I realize you learned to play chess under, let's say, less than ideal circumstances, but traditional rules are that you're quiet, like in a round of golf. Concentration is important, and it's proper etiquette to respect your opponent's ability to do just that."

"Ha," Nick blurted out "No, we never had silence in the Alert facility. If anything, while we played chess, the rest of the team would be watching HBO. Back then, at one am there was this channel that was basically nonstop hot ass chicks in a skintight onesie doing crazy ass aerobics that made the suit climb up the crack of their ass. I think it was called *Aerobicise*. Robert! Damn, those were some hot women. So yes, we had to learn to multitask. Shit, I was twenty-three! That was a world-class distraction. But if you need me to be silent, I can wait until it's my turn to ask the question."

The Director nodded. "Thank you. I would appreciate that."

"Yes, sir. Sorry, sir." Nick sat patiently for a few minutes and then closed his eyes and began quietly whispering the lyrics to *Papa was a Rolling Stone* by *The Temptations*.

"It was the third of September, that day I'll always remember, yes, I will."

The Director glared at Nick and moved his queen's pawn one move forward.

# CHAPTER EIGHTEEN

The Director cleared his throat as Nick began the third verse of the song.

"Hey Momma, is it true what they say that Papa never worked a day in his life?" he sang in a high soprano-like voice.

Nick opened his eyes. "Done? Already?" Looking at the board, he saw the queen's pawn moved forward one move. Nick smiled. "So would now be a good time to ask my question, sir, or shall I move first?"

"Are you prepared to move?" The Director asked skeptically.

"Sure. I can move and then ask you, or if you prefer, ask and then move. Dealer's choice."

"Please move first and then ask," The Director replied in a challenging tone.

"Okay, sure" Nick moved his queen's bishop pawn one move forward.

The Director's eyes narrowed, and he mumbled, "White moves pawn C.2, moved to C.3."

"What was that?" Nick replied.

The Director replied, "Your move. That was your move."

"Really? How does that work? C.2? What?"

"You might have noticed on the side of the board along the top and bottom are numbers, and along the sides are letters. This is how you can determine moves," The Director replied in an authoritative tone. "The numbers and letters are used by Grand Masters' to play a version of chess called *Blind Chess*. In *Blind Chess,* you're required to memorize the board. The players cannot touch or see the board. They must remember the board."

Nick blinked. "No shit? Totally by memory? Everything? Every move and counter move? That would have been rough with the hotties on HBO gyrating around in paper thin onesies. Damn!"

The Director nodded. "Yes."

"Okay, how about *Star Trek* chess? Have you ever played *Star Trek* chess?"

It was The Director's turn to blink. He leaned back and looked at Nick, perplexed. The man was a fool. Lacking all manners and social skills. He had no formal education past high school, and even then, The Director knew from his background research Nick had performed well below standards. By all standard measures, a complete failure.

"Not only have I never played it, I've never heard of it!" The Director replied.

"It is challenging," Nick replied. "Too bad we didn't meet under different circumstances. I could have taught you how to play." Nick smiled and thought silently, *we're playing right now, you cocksucker.*

The Director huffed; as if Nick could teach him anything. He said, "Yes, how unfortunate" in a barely veiled, condescending tone.

"No doubt." Nick continued. "Anyway, my question?"

The Director nodded and waved his hand in small circles. "Please, yes, get on with it. Ask the question!" He barely managed to hide his irritation.

Nick's eyes lit up like a small child. "Seriously? Awesome! Okay, so *Operation Neptune Spear.* What really happened?"

The Director was silent for some time, watching Nick. Finally, he answered, "What do you think happened?"

Nick was suddenly serious. "Listen, that whole raid was a cluster-fuck. First the plan was for SEAL Team Six to go into Pakistan, remove Osama Bin Laden, and then the official story would be he was taken out by a drone strike. You and I have had some experience with drone strikes. My house in Colorado is evidence of that. Jay was a mess, but he did survive. Imagine if that had been the result! Osama still alive and looking like a huge piece of Blue Whale foreskin! Anyway, so the official story has to change when the SEAL team crashes a Black Stealth helicopter and the new official story is to admit that SEAL Team Six went in and removed Osama Bin Laden. True?"

The Director said nothing but nodded.

"So here is where it goes south of reality. SEAL Team Six goes in and kills Osama because they fear he'll blow himself up. His multiple wives survive, however, and then the team has the time to remove all computers and paperwork for possible intelligence value. Then they scrap the helicopter, blow it up, I guess. Like, what a mess. This is SEAL Team Six, and they don't make these kinds of mistakes."

"What mistakes?" The Director asked.

"Killing the target. His continued life had the most intelligence value. Some panicked rookie shoots to avoid being blown up? Not possible. This is a seasoned SEAL team member. This bullshit might work for the general public, but sir, I've been on entry teams. They don't make this kind of mistake. It's part of the deal, the risk of being blown up was very real long before they entered the room Osama was actually in. I've seen the results of those suicide vests. The entire compound would have been leveled had Osama actually had one. To claim this was their fear is ridiculous. It states the obvious."

The Director was silent.

"And then there's the fact that not one of the women present, his three wives and children, has made a public statement. Why hasn't *Oprah* or *Ellen DeGeneres* picked up that story and had them on for an entire week of hand-wringing and 'I am woman, hear me roar' hand holding and singing as the crowds' sway side to side? The only account

I've found of them speaking at all is in the UK Telegraph, and that was half-ass. And then there's SEAL Team Six."

"What about SEAL Team Six?" The Director replied, his eyes narrowed, but Nick noticed he'd made no denial of anything Nick had asked.

Nick paused for a moment, took a deep breath and continued. "So the SEAL teams have a code of silence. They conduct raids all around the world when required, but they never discuss them. Period. This is engrained in them. A source of pride for every SEAL team member. Yet SEAL Team Six takes a page from the *Kardashians'* playbook. They write books, make appearances on daytime television, several of them claiming they were the real shooter and the others' claims are all lies. All that's missing are the sex tapes, trophy pic selfies with Osama's dead body and which team member secretly fell in love with Osama's wives after the raid. Seriously?"

The Director looked at his hands and spoke quietly, "And your question?"

Nick noticed The Director had still made no denial of his observations. A lack of denial, in Nick's world, was considered an admission. Nick spoke quietly, "I guess after seeing your response, or lack of response to my questions, is an answer of sorts."

The Director replied, "Now I have a question. What do you see happening after our little chess game comes to its end?"

It was Nick's turn to be caught off guard. "I expect to win the game and you'll stand down. End the camps and leave the team I've been working with alone. Let us be. We just want to be left alone. I want to be left alone."

The Director said nothing for some time and then returned to the game and moved another piece, taking one of Nick's pawns. Nick responded and took the pawn that had taken his, then The Director's knight took another pawn. Nick's bishop took the knight. The flurry of chess blows stopped, the façade of politeness was removed, and the reality of the deadly game's consequences was now clear. Nick had lost two pawns; The Director, a pawn and a knight.

Nick waited for the answer from The Director. If he agreed to leave Nick and the team alone if Nick won the game, Nick wasn't sure what he would do. The cost of the battle with The Director had been high, and Nick desperately needed peace. He wanted to know the team would be safe from any further attacks, but deep down he had to admit he'd known no other way to live for so long, for so many years before the mission to Baroota began; he had no idea how that would look.

The Director cleared his throat and smiled a carefree smile. "You have to understand that when this match has come to its inevitable end, with my victory, you'll be gathered up by the tactical team and ushered to one of the vehicles waiting. From there, your life will take a nasty turn for the worse." The Director paused and watched Nick for a response. There was none. "As far as the team of women you've surrounded yourself with. There will be nowhere they can run that I will not pursue them. They will pay dearly for crossing me. And your beloved Bexx? I will take great pleasure in personally breaking her. When I am done with her, if you somehow survived, you wouldn't be able to recognize her. She'll be walking the streets of Czech, sucking off random men for pennies. Then I'll reopen the missile facility under a new name. Camp Chakana. Things will return to normal in my world."

Nick clenched his teeth. He could reach across the table and crush this pricks throat before the two tactical team members or Ian could stop him. His breathing increased rapidly, and a tear rolled down his cheek. Nick nodded but said nothing for several minutes. The Director returned to the game and took another piece from Nick's side of the board. The Director saw the tear and knew he had finally beaten Nick, he realized the futility of his tactics and choice to meet and play this ridiculous game of chess.

Nick listened to The Director's response. Had The Director agreed to the winner takes all premise of the game, Nick wasn't sure whether he would've believed it. He wanted to believe it. Needed to believe it. Now that The Director's intent was clear, it was a tremendous relief. The tear The Director saw wasn't despair. It was relief. He was free to destroy The Director. Nick had asked The Director his strategy for the bigger match, and surprisingly he laid it out. Blow by Blow. Huge mistake.

Nick looked off to the left at the water running in the manmade pools. And tried to slow his breathing. The Director smiled watching the reality of Nick's position sinking in. That smart-ass façade was gone. No more singing, or ridiculous and distracting questions.

"Shall we continue the game, or would you like to concede defeat now?" The Director asked.

"Well since my continued play means I postpone near-certain torture and death, I guess the answer is obvious. Let's continue." Nick replied.

A moment later Nick said, "Why Chakana? I mean why rename it?"

"Why not," replied The Director. "It was the bottle next in line to be opened, you do remember the wine bottles don't you Nick?"

Nick nodded.

# CHAPTER NINETEEN

The match shifted gears. The Director felt he had the upper hand and planned on exploiting it. Immediately after that thought crossed his mind, he realized it also implied he hadn't felt he had the upper hand earlier in the match. That was disconcerting. He looked up at Nick as he scanned the potential moves on the chessboard. The Wild Card was an enigma. How had he wrestled control of the match from The Director? It was subtle, yet effective.

Bexx listened to the exchange between Nick and The Director and was suddenly struck by the reality of what The Director had said. There would be no peace for her or the team if he survived the game. All their lives hung in the balance. If Nick didn't kill The Director, he would be dead, probably in a few hours, and they would be hunted. She began typing on VSAT terminal.

*If Nick doesn't kill The Director, can you provide us with protection if we agree to the proposal?*

*I can't guarantee your safety if Director Taylor survives. He is a formable opponent. Meanwhile, I have a Chess Master who is monitoring the game. There are four possible moves left for Nick before he's in check. If you want me to even his odds of survival, you must act quickly. I have a team of experts trying to figure out his plan, and it baffles all of us. I see no way for him to defeat Director Taylor in the game, and there is no way he can kill Taylor if I don't interfere. I need your decision.*

Bexx sat back and thought for a moment. She didn't like feeling so out of control of her own destiny. If Nick killed The Director with her help, then she was committing the team to working for some random unknown government official. But if Nick died and The Director survived, she and the team would be hunted for life. Her destiny was in Nick's hands.

Bexx mumbled, "That crazy son of a bitch had better kill him." She'd made her decision.

*Make the move, even the odds. We're in. I agree to the proposal. However, should Nick survive, he's not to be part of the team. Period. That isn't negotiable. Are we clear on that point?*

*We're clear. Stand by.*

Nick scanned the board, counting how many possible moves he had left. Not many. Very few, to be honest. He'd never intended to win the game. He knew this was a one-way ticket, but he had to sell the show. The Director had to believe without a doubt that Nick wanted to end their conflict in a winner-takes-all game of chess. Nick leaned back up and stretched his arms, watching the tactical team's reaction to his movement. The guy on the left was watching his every move, hand still on the pistol grip of his issued MP-5, trigger finger dancing lightly on the trigger. He wore mirrored sunglasses, so Nick had no idea of his mindset, but judging from his body posture and itchy trigger finger, he'd seen some action somewhere. Guy on the right, not so much. His gun hand was off his weapon; he hadn't even reacted to Nick's movements. He was knuckle deep digging for gold in his nose. Nick thought, *Good, at least one is bored, one to fight when the shit breaks loose, but if he stays on trigger, I'm dead. Nothing equalizes a fight like a gun. Mike Tyson ain't shit when a .357 magnum starts to sing.* These guys had MP-5s. If Nick could get the booger hunting guard's gun, then the odds were equal. They were standing behind Ian, which would make it tough to reach them when the game came to its end.

Next, he checked Ian. Ian watched his every move; the guy's attention to his charge was meticulous, commendable even. He could use that to his advantage when the time came. When Nick made his move, Ian's concern for The Director would make him predictable, manipulatable.

Nick returned his attention to the board and moved a piece he knew he'd already lost to The Director and then watched as The Director settled in for the kill.

The Director saw Nick had very few moves left. The game was nearly over, and he had to be feeling anxiety. His time was nearly up. Finally, he would be disposed of and the team of Asgarda that had helped him would be crushed. The Director smiled content in the knowledge of his impending victory.

"It's nearly over, my friend. You have three moves left, three moves, and I will have defeated you."

Nick smirked. "Your chess game is lacking, sir. Lacking imagination, lacking enthusiasm, lacking passion. Check the board again, my friend. I have plenty of moves left."

The Director nodded. He'd seen this many times. An opponent who refused to believe they were defeated. Living in a dream world until the painful reality hit. The Wild Card had miscalculated and couldn't admit it to himself, much less his opponent.

Out of the corner of his eye, Nick saw both tactical team members reach for their earpieces. A communication was coming over the radio, and they were focused on it. He could move now and take advantage of their break in concentration. He may not get another chance. Nick picked up the flask and took a large volume of vodka into his mouth. As he watched the two tactical team members, he noticed they weren't paying attention to him. Now was the time.

He heard the guy on the left speak into a mic hidden somewhere in all his gear. "Say again, confirm that order?"

Nick stopped; something was happening the tactical team didn't expect. Confirming the order meant they had to be absolutely sure it wasn't misunderstood. Tactical teams don't hesitate, don't question. They do what they're trained to do without hesitation; hesitation kills. Nick spit the vodka back into the flask and watched. The tactical team members confirmed the order and looked at each other for a moment. They did a very military about face and walked away, heading back down the ramp. Nick was stunned and thought, *there's something you don't see every day!*

Nick's mind ramped up into hyperaware mode. The tactical team's action could mean only one thing: The Director had enemies, and those enemies had been watching. The odds of Nick's survival weren't exactly even, but they had improved immensely. Nick quickly checked to see if Ian had noticed the tactical team's departure; nope, his eyes were locked on Nick. Perfect.

Nick had three moves left on the chessboard. And two moves off. Time to play for keeps.

"Sir, I don't mean to tell you your game, but there's still time to reconsider. You're two moves from checkmate. I'd like to believe you're an honorable man on some level and would agree to leave me and the team of Asgarda alone when I win the match. There's still time, sir. Are you sure you won't reconsider? I mean, in my world karma is a bitch that has a long memory. Do you really want to be on the list of payback for wrongs committed to your fellow man even more than you already are?"

"I'll take my chances, Nick." The Director smiled. "Besides, seems to me karma has your name as well, and perhaps today she's come to collect."

Nick shrugged. "Could be."

"Sir, have you ever heard of *Chaos Theory?*"

The Director's eyebrows raised at the bizarre question. *Chaos Theory?* What the hell was Nick thinking now?

Behind Director Taylor, Ian was paying close attention; he could feel something had changed in Nick's demeanor. Sudden confidence, and a look in his eye. Whatever he'd planned, it was coming soon. Ian stood ready to protect The Director, even if it meant he'd be harmed or killed.

The Director finally commented, "No, Nick, never heard of it. Why?"

"*Chaos Theory.* It's a branch of mathematics that focuses on the development of dynamic systems. A bunch of confusing mumbo jumbo, I know, but in a nutshell, it deals with the weakness inherent in a complex system."

The Director was lost. This had nothing to do with anything. "Let's just play the chess game, Nick. We both know you've lost."

Nick shook his head. "See, that's just the problem. The more structured your play, the less you're able to see I play in an unconventional manner. You see, according to the game you play, I'm about to lose, but you have a blind spot, sir, and are nearly in checkmate."

The Director shook his head. "No, I'm going to win this game; we both know it. Make your move and quit stalling."

Nick smiled. "As you wish, sir." Nick picked up his flask and twisted off the cap. "You know, I was sitting in a tire shop in Grand Forks on my way here. I was having new shoes installed on the old beast I mechanically restored to make this trip. There was a daytime television show on in the waiting room. Very informative show, by the way. Some hot-tempered world-class chef teaching stay at home moms how to cook gourmet meals for their hard-working husbands."

The Director rolled his eyes; this would end soon enough. He thought, *I think I'll have his tongue ripped out first so he can no longer speak. This constant line of bullshit is tedious.*

Nick picked up the final piece he would move on the board. "Anyway, they were making this tasty dish called Vodka Pasta. Have you had it, sir?"

The Director's eyes darkened. "No. Can you make your move now?"

"Sure thing, sir." Nick moved the piece and placed it on the board. He announced, "Check and mate!" At the same time, he took a significant draw on the flask, sucking as much of the vodka into his mouth as he could. With the hand that had moved the last chess piece, he reached into his pants pocket and retrieved the Bic lighter.

Ian was stunned by Nick's claim he'd checkmated The Director. He leaned forward to see for himself if it was true.

The Director was stunned as well and looked down at the board. How could it be? He quickly examined the board and saw Nick had made an illegal move. He said, "No, you haven't checkmated me. That's an illegal move!"

Nick spit the entire contents of his mouth out in a fine mist that covered The Director in vodka and spit. "Wrong, sir, I win. Your king is in real jeopardy, sir. Shāh Māt!"

Nick lit the lighter and touched it to the chessboard where the vodka had sprayed. The entire table, chessboard and The Director erupted in a hot blue flame. Nick took another drag on the flask and spit it on The Director again, making sure he was engulfed.

"Arthur sends you his best, you son of a bitch."

# CHAPTER TWENTY

N ick sat back and watched calmly as Ian tried to understand what had just happened. First, Nick had called out check and mate. The Director had disputed the move and then erupted in flames. He had to do something, and quick, or The Director would die. Ian stepped forward and grabbed the handles on the rear of the chair and tried to pull it back towards him. His immediate plan was to get The Director to one of the water park's pools or fountains and get the fire extinguished. It was possible The Director could survive the fire if he could get it extinguished quickly. Ian pulled on the chair and it spun around, but the right rear tire was locked. He knelt quickly and reached his hand into burning flames to grab the manual brake and release it. His hand burned on the hot metal, but it would heal. When he stood up, Nick was immediately in front of him, his mouth closed and cheeks full, then Ian was immediately covered in vodka and just as quickly engulfed in flames. Nick had made his final move.

Ian's concern for The Director and his welfare evaporated instantly. He was now on fire. Panic controlled his mind. He tried to think...water! Get to the water! He tried to open his eyes and go in the direction of the nearest pond. It was in front of him, approximately ten meters away. He started moving as best as he could in that direction. Somewhere in the back of his mind, he heard Director Taylor screaming, or was that him? He wasn't sure, the pain he felt was indescribable. It felt like his face was melting, his eyes, lips and ears all dripping off his face in hot molten drips of cooked blackened flesh.

"Ian, my friend, where you headed? Now's no time to leave the party! Shit's just getting real!"

Nick tried to get to Ian before he cleared the rail and made it to the pond below, but Ian had adrenaline on his side. His speed was driven by survival. He cleared the rail in one flip and hit the water below with a sizzle. Nick watched as he came to the top of the water and began to float face down to the outlet for the falls. His body finally stopping, head and right arm hanging over the edge of the falls, Nick watched for a minute. Satisfied he was dead, he returned to The Director.

Nick sat back down in the chair and watched as Director Taylor made his last final feeble moves, and then his arms curled up to his chest, hands making fists, turned inward. Nick had seen the involuntary muscle contraction occur many times on many victims of a fire. The smell of the burning flesh was pungent, and normally it would have been offensive and sickening. Today, Nick reveled in it. Took it into his lungs and savored it.

"Fuck you," he finally said and got up.

Turning to the Tahoe caravan that had been waiting at the curb, Nick expected to be shot at any moment. Instead, the TAC team had gotten into the vehicles and were beginning to pull away from the curb. Nick watched and nodded as he watched them leave.

"Someone definitely wanted you dead as much as I did, you arrogant fuck. Karma has finally come calling."

Nick turned back to the flaming heap of what had been The Director, then he looked at Ian, his arm still hanging over the edge of the falls.

"Gentlemen, it's been real," Nick said as he began to walk down the ramp to the lower portion of the water park.

Bexx watched, stunned at the unexpected outcome of the meeting. Nick had won. Part of her wanted to scream in exultation. She watched as he attacked Ian and then as both men had been killed and within moments of each other. The audio feed had quit working a few moments after Director Taylor's chair had been engulfed in flames but not before she heard the screams of the now dying Director Taylor.

Bexx typed in the VSAT, *Looks like we're in business. We'll be leaving the facility here immediately. How will I contact you?*

*I'll contact you. Keep training and preparing. I would suggest you return to Moses Lake and assume ownership of the previous facility. I can secure the property title and take care of the details.*

Bexx thought about it. Moses Lake made sense. The Driver's home would be familiar territory; they knew the area, and they'd have access to a world-class runway and airport.

*Done,* she replied on the VSAT. *We'll be en route immediately.*

Bexx turned the VSAT off and secured the keyboard and then began climbing down the metal ladder that allowed access to the facility's rooftop.

"Asgarda on me," she announced when she entered the facility. When the team had gathered, she said, "We leave immediately. Make one last sweep through the facility and ensure we've left nothing we may need. I want to be on the road in thirty-minutes. Understood?"

As one voice, the team responded, "Yes, Commander."

"Are there any questions?"

Svetlana spoke up. "Yes, I have one. Is the chess match over?"

"Yes," Bexx responded.

Svetlana continued. "Who won?"

Bexx looked at her directly. "Does it matter? We're leaving. Let's go."

Svetlana pressed harder. She wasn't Asgarda and had never backed down to Bexx. "Yes, Commander, it matters. Did Nick win or not?"

Bexx turned, angered at the challenge to her position, glaring at Svetlana. Svetlana stared back. Bexx paused and then reconsidered her anger. Finally, she said, "Yes, Nick won. The Director is dead."

Svetlana asked, "Then where are we going, Commander?"

"To Moses Lake. We have a new mission."

As the Asgarda dispersed and checked the facility one last time, Bexx called to The Mentalist and Buffy individually. When The Mentalist arrived, she gave her a sealed envelope and told her to leave it in the first aid kit. Buffy received the same direction, but her envelope went in the Bat Cave. Two more envelopes were placed when the individual team members returned. Finally when Bexx was alone, she opened the armory and picked up the blocks of C-4 explosives, placing a sealed envelope on the shelf they were kept on. She then replaced the C-4, covering up the envelope, and closed and secured the armory.

"Time to go," she whispered quietly to herself. "Good luck."

Nick reached the street, turned left towards the hotel and began walking down Crystal Drive. There was no rush. He'd shower, shave and check out early. Time to go home.

As Nick walked down Crystal Drive, it immediately struck him that he hadn't noticed anything about the area. Just one block away was a *Jimmy John's*.

"Freaky fast," Nick said, smiling. "That's good because I'm freaky hungry and want to get on the road." He crossed the street and walked inside, waiting in the line to order because of the heavy lunchtime traffic. As Nick waited, he watched as a tall brown-haired woman wearing a business suit entered the restroom. Instantly, memories flooded back to him; the memory of another *Jimmy John's* and business unfinished. There had been another tall brown-haired woman in another *Jimmy John's* an entire lifetime ago. They had planned on a risky rendezvous in the woman's bathroom at lunchtime. Never happened; the timing was wrong, planets didn't align. *Weird*, Nick thought, *how critical timing was. Some relationships rolled along smooth; others are constantly banging up against each other like a car out of time, cylinders firing at the wrong time, car backfiring and sputtering. Timing mattered. That, and she was a demolitions expert, always blowing up the relationship just when it started to get real.*

Nick snapped back to the current *Jimmy John's*. "Sir, may I take your order?" the employee beckoned from behind the counter he realized now for the third time.

"Sorry, number ten, cut in half and a large drink."

"Would you like anything else?"

"No, that's good."

"Will that be to stay or to go?"
"To go."

Nick paid the amount required and grabbed his cup. By the time the cup had been filled with ice and a cold drink, the sandwich had been made and was waiting. Nick smiled, thinking, *Freaky fast.*

He turned and walked towards the door and took one last look at the long hallway leading towards the restrooms and smiled.

Outside, Nick started to walk towards the hotel, sipping the drink. Off in the distance, he could hear the sirens approaching. "Too late," he muttered. "Much too late. Nothing but worthless burnt meat there now."

Back at the hotel, Nick pulled open the door and walked into the lobby. The clerk Nick had thought he would never see again was still there, looking busy fussing over paperwork, tidying up pencils and pens.

Looking up and seeing Nick, the clerk nodded. "Back again, sir?"

"Yes, I'll be checking out early. Business ended well."

"Excellent, sir," the clerk spoke much too enthusiastically. "I'll prepare your paperwork. Which room was it again?"

Nick mentioned the room and continued walking as the clerk's continued speech slowly faded into the distance. He didn't want to hear any more bullshit from the pencil pushing clerk.

Once in the room, Nick stripped, took a long, hot shower, checked the bruises from the sucker punches the lead tactical officer had delivered and then shaved. Dressing in his own clothes, he ditched the second-hand clothes he'd purchased for the meeting with Director Taylor. Everything except for the field jacket, he liked how it felt to wear one again.

Back in the lobby thirty-minutes later, Nick stepped up to the counter and said, "Checking out."

The clerk didn't recognize him. "What room number, please?"

"Same room number I told you a half hour ago," Nick growled.
The clerk looked at him, puzzled, and then his face turned red. "Sorry, sir, didn't recognize you."

"Of course you didn't," Nick responded. "I didn't fit your neat and tidy expectations, then. Do I now?"

The clerk apologized and handed Nick the paperwork confirming he'd been checked out of the hotel. Nick turned and left the lobby, headed towards the parking terrace and the ancient F150. Nick unlocked the door, threw his small bag of clothes and the food on the front seat and hopped up in the truck. Turning the key breathed life into the waiting motor. The deep rumble of the *Magnaflow* mufflers echoed in the underground terrace. "Hello, sexy," Nick said, smiling, "ready to take me home?"

# CHAPTER TWENTY-ONE

T he trip home was slow going. There were a lot of construction zones on I-70, and freeway speeds dropped to thirty-five miles per hour.

*No bother,* Nick thought, *it isn't like there will be much to go home to.*

He was pretty sure Bexx would be gone when he arrived. If she was there, she wouldn't be happy with him. He had left with very little warning, if any, and by now her anger at his risk-taking would be full-blown fury. That was the best option. The worst was the facility would be empty, or even worse than that, Diamond Dave would remain behind and they'd set up a man cave.

"Ugh," Nick groaned out loud. Yes! That was the worst option. Keeping Diamond Dave around when The Director was alive was a nec-essary evil. Now? Tedious at best. There were worse things than being alone, and one was having an annoying roomie. Every enlisted man, college student, and missionary in the world knew that fact intimately.

Nick stopped at a small gas station at 106 N. Center Avenue in New Stanton, Pennsylvania, and filled up the F150's dual tanks with premi-um. Replacing the gas caps, he turned and headed into the small conve-nience store to get a drink and hit the head. Waiting in line to pay for the drink, he watched the overhead flat screen television. CNN was an-nouncing the latest updates in the world and local events. The announcer rambled on about random world news events Nick couldn't have cared less about. Syria was still an issue, Russia probe, Mueller investigation, blah blah blah, and then today in Virginia in a freak accident, Robert Taylor, the Director of both the *National Intelligence Agency* and *De-fense Intelligence Agency,* was killed. Director Taylor was playing chess at a favorite chess park when his wheelchair caught on fire. Witnesses say his personal assistant was present and tried to put out the fire and was nearly killed himself. The assistant, whose name has not been released, is in critical condition at a local hospital. He is not expected to survive the accident.

Nick thought, *Son of a bitch! Ian survived!*

Bexx stared out the window as the miles between her and the missile silo gradually increased. Special K was driving and occasionally smiled as she looked over at Bexx. At last, there was just the two of them again. She knew she could find a way to win Bexx back if she was patient. Now that Nick was out of the mix and Bexx was finished with him, their eventual reunification was inevitable in her mind. Behind her in the second seat of the van, Svetlana also watched Bexx but with a very different agenda in mind. Her eyes were critical and assessing. She looked Bexx up and down with an obviously disapproving glare and then turned and looked out her window. The van was incredibly quiet. No one spoke. There was no light chit-chat. The air was thick and heavy with anxiety. The team knew something more than just Nick defeating The Director had happened, but no one could put their finger on exactly what it was. Something had changed; they could feel it.

The rest of Nick's trip back to Dresden, North Dakota, occurred without incident. He arrived at the missile facility after twenty-six hours of nearly continuous driving. When he arrived, it was nearly six pm local time. The drive had passed remarkably quickly as his mind replayed the events at the water park over and over again. Finally, he pulled up to the military grade chain link fence and got out to unlock the gate. The land around the facility was quiet. There were no signs of anyone being near. Opening the gate, he drove in a few meters and then stopped the old truck.

"We're home, girl, good job," he muttered as he patted the weathered paint on the back of the truck.

Nick locked the gate and returned to the truck and drove into the three-car garage. It was empty, completely void of any vehicles. Nick remained in the truck for a moment, suddenly aware he was exhausted, and muttered, "Shit, she's gone. Definitely gone."

Nick picked up the bag from the floor of the truck and took his clothes inside the facility. The building was incredibly quiet. The only sounds were his footsteps echoing through the large empty space. Walking to what had been their room, he got undressed and crawled into bed. The sheets smelled like her scent, and he wrapped up in them and closed his eyes. This was part of the deal when you entered into any relationship. The beginning, the middle, and the end. The end was what he experienced now. The loss. He knew soon enough the pain would pass and he would begin to heal, but for now, the hurt was very real. Nick rolled over on his back and opened his eyes and began tracing the metal conduit on the ceiling.

Nick woke up and remembered where he was, back in the facility; the silence was deep and ominous. He closed his eyes and listened for any noise, anything at all to indicate movement in the facility. The loudest noise he could hear was his own heart, slowly, methodically beating. The surge of blood through his veins made his body slightly rock under the sheets. That was the only noise he could hear, his skin gently moving against the sheets. He threw the sheets back and began the day. First order of business, he checked the armory. See what weapons were left, ammo, etc. The battle with Director Taylor was over, but that didn't mean his life would change. This, he understood. It could never change. When you're born a wolf, the idea of any other way of living is unimaginable.

Nick unlocked the armory and accessed the cache Bexx had left. Only the hand-held weapons were missing, swords, knives, etc. The C-4 was still there. He stared at it momentarily, then removed it from the shelf. Underneath was an envelope. He picked it up and opened it.

*N, in the facility there will be four envelopes. Each sealed and empty. I need to know if any are missing or opened. If they're opened or missing, tell me where you found them. Send a letter general delivery, Moses Lake, signature required to my real name, Tamriko Bzikadze. Wish me luck, T*

Nick smiled. A double-blind, that way no one would know anything from the contents. The message was in the location and condition of how and where the envelopes were found. Maybe there was still hope? Nick checked the facility and found two of the letters unopened and noted their location. One he found opened in the gym, the other in a garbage can torn into three pieces. Nothing he could do from here. This was her's to deal with, this had been their arrangement. Deceive the deceivers.

Nick removed the C-4 and began the preparations. The traitor's continued deception meant only one thing: he had to be ready for that end.

Once the facility security had been complete, Nick showered and prepared to make the short trip to the post office. This would become part of his daily ritual, workout, shower and check the post office. Then lunch at the attached café. Routine helped make the day pass, provided structure where no structure existed. Nick understood now what it was like for Bexx to wait and be unable to take action.

The following morning, the team arrived at Moses Lake. Bexx and Special K conducted a sweep of the farmhouse to ensure it was safe for the rest of the team to enter, then they went to the barn. A thorough search of the barn was completed, and it was found to be secure and free of booby traps. Bexx looked in the stall that had been Lennie's. It was empty and exactly as she remembered. What had Nick called her? The forensic proctologist? Bexx smiled; Nick had a way of reducing the most intimidating and hard-earned titles and degrees to shreds of humiliating reminders of your overinflated ego in a single sarcastic breath. Special K watched Bexx as she looked at the empty stall.

"Lots of room there if, say, you were interested in revisiting some past indiscretions and perhaps creating some new ones."

Bexx smiled. "Indiscretions? Is that what it was? Do you know what that means? We were displaying a lack of good judgment? Is that how you saw it?"

Special K closed the gap between them. "Perhaps I like the idea of you not being so in control and making such careful and calculated decisions. Perhaps indiscretion to me meant Bexx was a little bit out of control and not caring for a moment about the consequences of her actions."

Bexx smiled. "Perhaps," she said. "Come on, let's go check out the rest of the outbuildings before we…"

"Before we what?" Special K interrupted, asking coyly.

"Come on, Miss Flirty flirt, let's go get moved in," Bexx said, smiling, and turned to walk out of the barn. Her face turned from a smile to deadly serious in an instant.

# CHAPTER TWENTY-TWO

W hat was supposed to be one, maybe two weeks - okay, three if it all went to shit - was now three months. Bexx was supposed to take the team if Nick survived his meeting with The Director and weed out the two traitors he'd discovered on the missile facility rooftop. That had been his recommendation. Three months ago, he returned to the missile facility and she'd taken the team and left. There's an old saying that absence makes the heart grow fonder; that was never the case in Nick's life experience. Reality was, absence made the heart go wander. Bexx was gone; it was that simple. What'd happened? Nick didn't know...maybe the traitors got the best of her? If that was so, she was gone as well, dead. If she changed her mind, there was no point in pressing her anymore. She'd left the note and asked him to let her know about the envelopes. He'd done that, and he waited, checking the post office daily for any return message. None came. Nothing, not even a goodbye or I changed my mind, sorry and good luck. He was cut off, completely isolated, and by her choice.

At first, the depression was crushing. Nick slept, ate, and rarely bathed. Walking the halls of the facility, pacing, moving without purpose. Movement itself was all he could manage. Move to stay alive. Walking back and forth, pacing. The mindless contraction of the leg muscles and arms slightly swinging slowly burned off the excess energy generated by the toxic life-extinguishing anxiety. Suicide floated in the back of his mind, making its familiar reappearance on the edges of his peripheral mental vision. Movement where none should be, and when you turn to see what it was, you see nothing, but you knew it was there taunting you. Suggesting a permanent solution to a temporary problem.

*Let's dance one last dance, Nick.*

Thankfully, the darkness started to lift, bit by bit. The mental clouds lifted, the daily movement became purposeful again and the heavy feeling in his chest started to lighten.

Every two days, exactly every forty-eight hours the alarm went off on his cell phone and he stepped onto the *VersaClimber*. Working through twenty-minutes of hell had kept him sane. Several times, he'd nearly said to hell with it and sat at the bottom of the Versa and waited. He'd set a timer that could only be reset by a twenty-minute workout on the machine. Twenty-minutes, and the timer reset, the C-4 charges remained intact, detonation postponed for another two days. He tied the suicide blast to the Versa because no one would roll through twenty-minutes on that machine on a whim. It was a ball buster, even for the most fit. It was his insurance policy. One final defiant act, should the reality of his life return and someone came knocking with the intent to do him harm. That would be a big mistake. Clinically, he would easily be diagnosed paranoid and depressed, suicidal, yes, all of it accurate.

Nick would respond to the diagnosis, "It's only paranoia if you aren't being hunted." He'd been hunted for too long to change now.

In Moses Lake Bexx and Special K had finally reconnected. It hadn't been an easy thing for Special K to win her back. It took work, time and trust, and to be honest, a lot of manipulation. But Special K was determined to have her soulmate back in her life, and finally Bexx had relented. For Special K, it was like life had finally started to flow favorably in her direction. Things finally had turned around, and the months of keeping her mouth shut and jealousy in check while she watched Nick and Bexx were just a painful memory, growing pleasantly more distant every day.

The daily routine at Moses Lake had returned to nearly the same routine as before the move. Morning runs led by Special K, followed by combat training in the barnyard. Meals prepared by each team member as they took a turn. Several mentioned quietly that they missed JT's cooking. They'd become accustomed to his regime of healthy food, which tasted exceptional. Svetlana watched as the team returned to what had been their normal routine. She participated in the morning runs and combat training and surprised more than one member of the team with the skill set JT had instilled. She'd been a quick study and immediately had taken to improvising what she'd learned. Bexx was happy with her progress as a member of the team. She would prove to be a valuable asset should she choose to join their ranks. Whether that actually happened or not remained to be seen. It also remained to be seen if she could get along with Bexx as their leader. Their relationship had been tense since they left the facility. Svetlana constantly asked questions and challenged the status quo. She had not been in a military environment and had no military training. Prior to her abduction, she hadn't asked a lot of questions of anyone. She tried to be friendly, pleasant and accommodating. That person had died when she'd been abducted and forced into sexual slavery.

One day, Bexx called the team together in a group and began a briefing. They had been given a new assignment. Her communication with the anonymous person with knowledge of her past had continued off the VSAT. After receiving definite confirmation of The Director's death, there had been no need to purge the team of the two members who had been spying for him. Bexx explained she'd been aware they'd been infiltrated but had taken no action against the two anonymous spies. They needed to heal as a team and move forward. Besides, Nick had invited known associates of The Director into the compound and knowingly worked with them. She invited the two spies to come forward and explain their position. The team remained silent.

Finally, Special K stood up and admitted she'd been one of the spies. She explained that The Driver had offered her a way to win back her relationship with Bexx. At first, she was reluctant but then decided she would do anything to win back their relationship, even join in with The Director. She apologized to the team and Bexx and finished her confession with a tear-filled admission to Bexx.

"I love you, and I'd do anything to be with you. I'm sorry if I disappointed you."

The rest of the team was silent. Special K sat down and stared at the ground for several minutes and then at Svetlana.

Svetlana was stunned at Bexx's admission that she knew about the spies. Even more so that Special K had admitted what she'd done. They'd agreed never to admit what she'd done to Bexx or anyone on the team. Especially when Nick had been present. If Nick had known, it was pretty clear what would have happened almost immediately. Now that he was gone, it seemed wise just to let it go, drop it. Special K was no longer working for The Director and had rekindled her relationship with

Bexx. What could be gained by admitting her deception? Svetlana was furious.

Special K finally spoke up as she maintained the knowing eye contact with Svetlana. "Well, sis? Do you have anything you'd like to say?"

Svetlana had to think fast. Special K had forced her hand. She had to make an admission to save face with the team; it was now or never.

"I was the other person you're referring to," she said loudly, locking eyes with Bexx. "Special K told me what she'd done, and I agreed to keep her secret. I didn't work for The Director, but I knew of her collusion. I had no other motive than that. I just wanted to keep her safe. Period. Family first; she is my sister."

Bexx nodded. She'd suspected as much, but with the team back in a place where they could work as one unit, and not under the toxic influence of Nick's paranoid mentality, she was willing to move on.

"Are we agreed, then, that this is behind us?"

Special K nodded and said, "Yes, I am."

Bexx asked the remaining team members their opinions, and all agreed it was time to move on as one unit.

Bexx asked Svetlana specifically, "Can we put this behind us?"

Svetlana said nothing for several minutes, locking eyes with Bexx. "Yes," she finally said quietly.

Bexx released the rest of the team and asked Svetlana and Special K to remain behind.

"As you know, we have a new benefactor, and a new mission. We've been tasked with a mission that's delicate, to say the least. It requires infiltration of a hardened facility and the subsequent submission of a high-value target. I'm asking for volunteers. But before either one of you says a thing, understand if the mission goes south, or you're discovered, you'll most definitely be killed. There'll be no back-up, you'll be on your own."

Special K asked when the mission would begin.

Bexx answered, "Training will begin immediately. When the volunteer feels they're ready, they'll leave. The rest of the team will stay behind, unaware of the true nature of the mission."

"And the high-value target, who is it?" Svetlana asked.

Bexx answered, "Does it matter? We're a team of mercenaries. We've been hired to do a job. If the identity of the target changes your feelings about the mission, then perhaps you shouldn't volunteer."

Svetlana felt her anger rise, her face now hot and red. Her loyalty to the team was directly questioned. She decided to take a chance.

"No, it doesn't matter. I'll volunteer for the mission."

Bexx looked at her, assessing her commitment. "Are you absolutely sure?"

"I am. I've made my decision. I volunteer."

"As you wish, then." And Bexx began to describe the mission in detail to both of them.

When she was done, Special K beamed with delight. The target was Nick.

# CHAPTER TWENTY-THREE

Bexx continued, speaking now directly to Svetlana. "As you can see, this will require some finesse, and I obviously can't be the one who makes direct contact with Nick. He'll know immediately something is wrong. Do you have a suggestion on how we should proceed?"

Svetlana thought for a moment. "I do. I suggest we have a direct conflict that ends in a physical confrontation between us. It must be in front of the team. When it's over, I'll leave. I must be marked by the fight for it to be believable. When I leave, you'll wait for my contact on the VSAT with the benefactor, who will then contact you to let you know I've been successful. If I fail and Nick kills me, you can then use that to motivate the entire team to proceed as one and take him out."

Bexx liked the plan and was a bit taken back by the absolute ruthlessness of it. Svetlana was becoming more formidable each day. Perhaps one day, the time would come when they would do battle in earnest. She needed to be prepared for that possibility.

Bexx nodded. "And when would you like this confrontation to occur?"

Svetlana responded, "Better if I decide and you have no idea. Your reactions will be more honest and realistic that way. More believable, don't you agree?"

Bexx nodded, showing no emotion. She had to admit, she now felt alarmed. Svetlana was maneuvering her skillfully.

"As you wish. Make it so," she finally responded.

Bexx stood up and walked away from Svetlana and Special K. She needed to make preparations for the rest of the team should Svetlana fail. As she walked, a thought occurred to her, and she smiled.

*Yes, that works nicely,* she thought and kept walking.

Two days later, the confrontation occurred.

Bexx was directing the team in some rigorous hand to hand combat training when Svetlana spoke up. "Tell me, Commander, how is it you expect our unquestioning loyalty and you leave one of our own behind without so much as an explanation?"

Bexx paused, confused. "What? Who are you referring to? Who have I left behind?"

"Nick! You left Nick. Without so much as a goodbye or an explanation, you just left. Maybe the rest of you have forgotten or are too afraid to speak up, but I would still be a slave to The Director, a sexual slave, tortured and used if it weren't for Nick. How is it that none, not one of you look back and wonder if we're doing the right thing by abandoning him?" Svetlana glared at the rest of the team. "You're all cowards. I'm disgusted at the sight of you. Nick saved us over and over again, and all it takes is for Bexx to quit sleeping with him and end their relationship and then say we're leaving, and you all drop everything and follow. You aren't mercenaries, you're sheep!" Svetlana spit on the ground in front of Bexx. "You make me sick to my stomach. You're a conniving bitch."

Bexx was angry. Even if this was a ploy, she was convinced Svetlana meant what she said and realized even more now that Svetlana was formidable.

Bexx approached her and spoke quietly and menacingly. "We settle our disputes in the ring. Since we have no ring here, we use hay bales. Are you challenging me to combat?"

Svetlana stepped towards her, "If you have the stomach for it, Commander, or would you have someone else on the team do your fighting for you? Seems to be your habit lately."

Bexx was livid. "Make it so. Now!" she yelled at the team. "Form the ring with hay bales," then she turned to The Mentalist, "get your medical bag. I have a hunch you'll need it."

Special K wasn't sure who to cheer for, Bexx or Svetlana. In the end, she sat silent, alarmed at the brutality of the fight. The two women stripped to the waist as was the Asgarda custom and entered the ring. Svetlana had been trained by JT and had been a quick study, while Bexx had many years of actual combat under her belt. She'd been challenged a few times in the past, and the fights had ended quickly. She'd always overpowered her opponents with her size and strength. Bexx smiled as she saw Svetlana's hands shaking. She would end this quickly. The Mentalist began the match, and the two women circled each other, looking for an advantage. Finally, they came together, and the battle began.

Thirty-minutes later, both Bexx and Svetlana were bloody. Hair had been pulled out by the handful by each of them. Bexx had expected a show for the team, and Svetlana gave her one and more. Bexx's left eye was swollen shut, and her nose bled a steady drip, drip, drip, down her chest. It was probably broken. No one had ever broken her nose before. Patches of her head were now bald, the hair ripped out and on the ground at her feet. Svetlana wasn't much better off. One eye was shut. The other closing rapidly; soon she would be blind, her nose was bloody but not broken. Both women were covered with angry, bloody scratches and bite marks. Svetlana had one broken finger on her left hand. The two women stood for a moment and glared at each other, the false pretense of the fight long forgotten.

Svetlana spit on the ground at Bexx's feet. "Fuck you! I'm done with you and your Asgarda! Fuck all of you!" She turned and left the circle, dressing as she walked away.

The team was quiet, stunned by the brutality of the fight. No one had ever held their own with Bexx, much less come to what most felt quietly was a definite draw. Additionally, the seeds Svetlana had planted with her speech had taken root. The team now doubted Bexx and her motives.

The Mentalist treated Bexx's injuries first, then when she was patched up, she went to Svetlana. It took some coaxing, but she convinced Svetlana to allow her to treat her injuries, set her broken finger and treated both swollen eyes. The Mentalist said nothing while she treated Svetlana's injuries except to ask where she hurt and if there were any injuries she'd missed treating. Svetlana shook her head no. When

The Mentalist was done, she left Svetlana's room, closing the door.

Special K accompanied Bexx to their room, the same room that had previously been Nick and Bexx's. She closed the door and tried to help Bexx, treating her injuries, talking quietly to her. Handfuls of her black hair fell to the floor as Special K tried to comb out the blood clots and dirt. Finally, Special K said, "So was that what you expected when you planned this operation with Svetlana?"

Bexx said nothing. Her pride was hurt, and she realized again, she'd underestimated Svetlana. She basically gave her permission for the fight and expected Svetlana to fight in a convincing manner. She hadn't expected a street brawl, and she definitely had not expected Svetlana to inflict this kind of damage.

Once Svetlana was able to see well enough to drive, she began to pack her clothes. She asked Special K to take her to Moses Lake, and they went looking for a good used car. Perhaps it was coincidence or providence, neither knew for sure, but they found an old Toyota truck for sale, four-wheel drive, stick shift, five speed. The miles didn't matter.

Svetlana said to Special K, "That's it. That'll be my first in with Nick. The truck." They purchased the truck and drove it to the nearest tire shop, a *Les Schwab* full-service station. New tires, oil change, and an alignment were recommended by the technicians there. Svetlana gave the okay, and the repairs were completed. When she was ready, she turned to Special K and smiled.

"Take care, sis. Tell Bexx I'm on my way to North Dakota. Next stop, the missile facility! Wish me luck. Tell her I'll contact the benefactor on the military grade VSAT when I have Nick subdued."

The two women hugged, and Svetlana climbed into the cab of the truck and closed the door. Grinding the first gear, she smiled sheepishly at Special K and forced the transmission into gear, then let out the clutch. The truck lurched forward and died.

"So much for the dramatic goodbyes," Svetlana said, laughing as she started the truck again. "Once more, dear sister?"

Svetlana smiled and laughed, her face still purple from the beating Bexx had given her. She eased the clutch out slowly and revved up the motor. The truck eased forward slowly, and Svetlana was off. A few more gears grinding metal on metal and the truck lurching forward, and Svetlana was on the interstate, headed back to North Dakota.

While Svetlana was hitting the road to Dresden, North Dakota, on her first mission as an Asgarda, Bexx had taken one of the vans and headed into Moses Lake herself. She stopped at the post office and dropped a letter into the slot outside in the lobby. The letter was addressed to Nick Hudson, General Delivery, Dresden, North Dakota. Inside the envelope was a letter warning Nick that Svetlana had been discovered as one of the spies and she could possibly be headed his direction. Bexx smiled as she turned and prepared to walk out of the post office. Her injuries already felt much better.

"Good luck with Nick! Now, who's the conniving bitch, you conniving bitch?!" Bexx whispered to herself as she opened the lobby door and exited the building.

# CHAPTER TWENTY-FOUR

Nick pulled into the post office for what felt like the millionth time; there would be nothing there. He knew if the definition for insanity was doing the same thing over and over and expecting a different result, well, he was insane. He had no choice; eventually, he knew he'd probably give up on her. But not yet, he couldn't; hope was usually a good thing. For Nick, hope was an empty syringe of heroin. There would be no high, no relief from the pain. Just a needle and an empty syringe, worthless. Because hope was like that, empty and dark when there were no results.

Nick got out of the F150, closed the door and went into the post office. The postal clerk heard the door open and smiled. Finally, she had a letter for the strange guy who came every day at noon, checked his box and then asked about general delivery.

"Was there anything there today?"

She nodded to Nick as he entered the post office. She held the letter and waited for him to check the PO box he'd purchased. She heard the small metal door open and a deep breath, then a sigh. Nothing again. He closed the door to the box and locked it, then walked past her and nod-ded.

"See you tomorrow," Nick said.

The clerk smiled. "Aren't you going to ask about general delivery today?" Nick heard as he walked to the door.

"Don't see any point in asking," he responded. "We both know there isn't anything there." Nick turned and smiled, a bleak, painful attempt at a smile.

The postal clerk held up a letter and waved it back and forth. "This letter came this morning. I've been waiting all day for you to come in." She smiled. "I hope it's what you've been waiting for."

Nick paused and looked at the envelope. If the postal worker was playing a prank on him, it was a dangerous prank. He hoped she had the sense not to do anything that foolish. His self-control was at the very edges of anything resembling safe. He knew that. One false step and Nick would redline, blow a gasket and rip someone apart for no reason.

Nick walked to the counter, and the clerk, sensing no danger, handed him the envelope and said, "I hope it's good news." She just turned away and walked back into the amazingly large warehouse part of the post office.

Once again, the thought occurred to Nick, how in the hell does such a small building from the outside look so large on the inside?

Nick glanced at the letter and saw it was in fact addressed to him, Nick Hudson. Not his false name, but the real one. If it was from Bexx, why didn't she send it to the box? He looked at the postmark and saw it was from Moses Lake, Washington. Nick put the letter in his jacket pocket and walked to the small convenience store attached to the post office.

The convenience store was small, and the only grocery store for the area. It also had a small café area. Nick's daily trips into the thriving metropolis of Dresden, North Dakota, had included a daily ritual of ordering lunch from the café. Nick walked into the café, and the cook took a deep breath. Something about the strange, quiet man was unsettling. The business could definitely use the money he spent on groceries and his daily burger and fries. However, he never changed the order; it was the same every day. He sat in the same chair at the same table and ate, then he would stare out the window; the stare was what bothered the cook. It was empty. His eyes looked like shark's eyes, they looked but did not see, and he rarely blinked. She timed it one day, and after five-minutes of not even the slightest flutter of an eyelid, she quit. He gave her the creeps.

"The usual, sir?"

Nick nodded yes but said nothing, pulled out his wallet and laid down a ten-dollar bill. Same every day; ten-dollar bill, keep the change.

The cook nodded and pulled out the usual bottle of Bud Light Lime in a longneck glass bottle. Twisting off the cap, she handed it across the counter and said, "The rest will be coming right up."

Nick nodded and then pointed at the restroom. "Be just a minute, okay?"

The clerk was stunned. Nick hadn't said a word in months. Day after day, meal after meal, not a word.

"Sure, take your time," she replied. "I'll put the meal on hold, so your food will be hot. When you come back out, I'll start the burger. Sound good?"

Nick nodded, then walked to the restroom. The picture on the door showed both sexes, no single gender bathrooms here in Dresden. Nick smiled. The shit people get spun up about amazed him. He opened the door and stepped into the small bathroom. Closing the door, he locked it and took out the letter. He needed someplace safe to read it, someplace no one would be able to see the look on his face. He knew what the letter would say, *Sorry, things changed once I left. You know I'd prefer if we were together, but well, I have the team, and they need me. Take care of yourself.*

Nick looked in the mirror and stared at his own face long and hard, then opened the envelope. Inside there was one piece of paper. He unfolded it and read the note Bexx had sent.

He looked on the other side of the paper and said, "That's it? No, fuck you, Nick, loser asshole. I'm never coming back. Good riddance."

Just some lame ass warning about Svetlana? Seriously, if she was one of the traitors, why the hell didn't you take care of it? Nick thought. This made no sense. Nothing for three months, and then heads up, Svetlana is on her way, please take care of her, sorry I dropped the ball here, been too busy finger banging with Special K. What the hell?

Nick crushed the paper and envelope in his hand and mumbled, "Fuck you, bitch. I don't hear dick from you, you cut me off, and now, fix this?" Nick looked in the mirror and said out loud, "Fuck you!" Jesus, why did every woman he was with have to be a demolitions expert? "They must teach that shit in sixth-grade sex education" Nick changed his voice into his best schoolmarm imitation and began the mock lesson. "And finally, girls, after you seduce him emotionally and sexually, here's how you blow shit up and really fuck with his head," Nick said angrily, glaring into the small bathroom mirror.

Outside the café, a Toyota four-wheel drive truck pulled up. The single occupant got out and walked to the post office and then came out a short moment later and headed to the café. The door opened, and the chime above the door rang out, announcing the entrance of another customer. A tall, athletic woman entered the café.

The cook turned and said, "Welcome. May I prepare a meal for you, ma'am?"

"Yes. First, is there a man in here, fifties, salt and pepper hair, exceptionally fit, doesn't talk much?"

The cook nodded and pointed at the restroom. "He's in there."

"Good. Did he order?"

"Yes, same thing every day, bacon burger, fries and a Bud Light Lime, bottle only. Has to be a longneck, or he won't drink it."

"Great. Make it two. Where does he sit?"

The cook stopped cooking. "Ma'am, it's none of my business, but I think you might want to reconsider. No one talks to him, no one sits with him. He doesn't seem like the sort that will appreciate a break in his routine if you take my meaning."

Svetlana nodded and said firmly, "Make the meals, serve them. I'll take care of the rest. Where does he sit?" It wasn't a request; it was a demand.

The cook was suddenly aware the woman had an air about her. A sense of confidence that was a bit disconcerting. She had a smile that barely covered a threatening demeanor, and her face was bruised and battered. Her left hand had a small splint on one of the fingers. She'd recently either been in a fight or a car wreck. Either way, the café suddenly felt dangerous to the cook.

"He sits there by the window, alone," the cook reiterated. "Always alone."

"Got it." Svetlana smiled again. "Alone, but not today."

Svetlana grabbed the two beer bottles and walked to the table and waited for Nick to return from the restroom. She'd decided from her past encounter with Nick, there was only one way this day would end well. She had to be entirely honest with him. If he got one whiff of anything deceptive, he'd probably kill her where she sat. The next few minutes would be intense and frightening. The longer she kept him calm, the better her chances. She took a deep breath and slowly let it out, blowing long and slow until her lungs completely emptied.

Nick unlocked the door to the restroom and stepped out into the café. There was a woman sitting at his table and two beers on the table, one in front of her, one across from her. Nick looked at the cook questioningly.

The cook looked back and pointed the flat metal flipper at the woman and shrugged as her eyebrows raised, sending the quiet nonverbal message, I don't know who she is, but she's here for you.

Nick nodded and did a quick visual check of the woman for weapons; her hands were in her jacket pockets, no noticeable bulges in the coat or at her ankles. If she was armed, it was something small. She wore boots, probably steel toe, weapons themselves in a pinch.

Nick walked up behind her quietly and spoke in a low, clear voice. "Hands on the table and they better be empty, or you die right here, right now. Understand, Svetlana?"

Svetlana nodded. She hadn't heard Nick open the door to the restroom or walk across the floor. She smiled; he still moved like a predator in the night. Slowly, she took her hands out of her pockets and spread her fingers, then placed them flat on the table, fingers splayed open.

"What happened to the finger on your left hand?" Nick asked.

"Bexx broke it before she sent me here to kill you," Svetlana replied.

"What?" Nick said, stunned.

# CHAPTER TWENTY-FIVE

S vetlana asked, "Do you think we could eat first? I haven't eaten in twelve hours, and this burger actually looks good. The story I have to tell you won't be easy to hear."

"What makes you think I'll listen?" Nick replied, his hand still holding the letter Bexx had sent. It felt real, her warning had arrived just in time. "Maybe I just kill you right here. You say she sent you here to kill me; maybe this is just the beginning of the ruse, the line of shit you came to sell. Listening means weakness, Svetlana. I learned that the hard way from The Driver. You feed me a line of shit, and while I work it out, you attack. Seems like I have nothing to gain by listening to your manipulative line of shit. You picked a public place to meet me for a reason. You wanted the safety of witnesses being present, am I right?"

"I did choose to meet you here, yes. I've been here for a couple of hours, waiting for you to come to the post office. I'd figured out Bexx must have had some way of communicating with you, if she was at all. I realized she knew there were spies on the team, and if she knew, you knew. I was one of those spies. I had to be."

Nick's breathing increased. Here was one of the spies he saw on the roof of the facility, feeding The Director intelligence on their plans. Because of her, he had to go at The Director with no plan, no backup, and hope for the best. It had worked out in the end, but the risk was extreme.

"You were on the roof, on The Driver's VSAT? You and one other. Who was with you?"

Nick watched her eyes as she realized he'd been there too, watching in the dark. Svetlana shivered as the reality hit her. He could have killed her then, but something stopped him.

"Yes, I was on the roof, with Special K. I had to be."

Nick growled, "I should kill you now. You betrayed me after everything that's happened, you turned against me, against us."

"There was no other way, please listen!" Svetlana pleaded.

Nick picked up his burger. "Eat, now! It may be your last meal. Enjoy it. Think hard about what you have to tell me, make sure you tell the truth. The slightest hint of a lie and I'll gut you right here. I'll watch the life fade from your eyes, and I'll enjoy it. Eat!"

Nick ate his burger, thinking as he went. She had to have a plan. She didn't have to take this tack. If Bexx had sent her, she could have disobeyed orders and just taken off. Never face him. If the Bexx story was a lie, why come at all? The Director was dead. None of it made sense. Her best bet was to jump ship and leave it all behind if Bexx had, in fact, sent her.

"First, why did Bexx break your finger and then send you here?"

"It's a long story," Svetlana replied as she took the first bite of her burger. "Short version, she wanted to sell to the team that I was on your side and mad she'd left you. I guess to see who had more loyalty to you than her. A test. What she didn't realize is I'd been watching her for some time. Special K, too. So, when she offered the job to me…" Svetlana paused. "Let's start at the beginning okay?"

Nick nodded and held up his hand and made a rolling motion, implying go ahead.

"Remember our last trip to this post office? I came to you and told you about the keylogger on my computer. I asked if it was there for a reason, and you were honest with me. It was because you suspected me as a plant, one of The Director's people because my story didn't add up. Remember?"

Nick nodded yes.

"So, when you came clean and told me the truth, I told you what I'd learned. The Driver was a spy and had been feeding The Director information. He'd actually been working for The Director for some time, and you just fell in his lap. By pure luck, you'd survived their attempts to kill you. I had to earn your trust and prove myself then. I'll do that now. First, in my search of The Driver and The Director's correspondence, I found out The Driver had used me to draw you out, and I thought punish my sister for helping kill Oelsen Hauer. We all thought that, remember?"

Nick nodded and stopped eating.

"We were wrong. She suggested they abduct me. She set me up. Imagine for a minute what my life would have been like if you and the team failed in Vegas. That was a very real possibility, your failure. Just another random decision you made at the last minute saved the entire team and rescued me from a life in hell. My sister did that! Let that sink in. What was her motivation?"

Nick put down his burger. It was starting to make sense. "She wanted Bexx and was willing to sacrifice all of us and you to make that happen? Seriously?" he asked.

Svetlana nodded.

"Why didn't you tell me?"

"I could see your focus was on The Director. Laser-like focus, very effective in defeating him, not in seeing your own weakness. You need-ed me to be your second pair of eyes and ears. To pick up what you'd missed. You were lucky after Baroota. Twice you defeated him. Three times would be unlikely. I heard all about the firewood incident, cutting wood until your hands were raw, bloody meat to gain back the edge Bexx had dulled. It made sense. She thinks differently. She is a merce-nary; do you realize that? No matter what your feelings for her may be, she isn't like you. She hunts for money; you joined this fight for pay-back. Originally, Baroota was payback. I figured that out, for what had been done to you. Am I right?"

Nick said nothing.

She stared at him for several moments, seeing she'd touched on something deep and painful.

Finally, she continued. "I realized you were driven by a very different motivation than the rest of the team. My sister used me as bait to draw you and Bexx back into this fight. She wanted Bexx to come to her aid and needed you to be wholly committed to the fight again. She put me in sexual slavery to draw you out. She knew when you found out what had happened, you'd be drawn in like a moth to a flame. You wouldn't be able to resist."

Nick sat motionless, listening, pieces falling into place in his head.

"Fast forward. I read this with my own eyes and realized we, you and I, were being played by her in a very complex game of manipulation. The team was never supposed to succeed. I was never going to be rescued. When it failed, and I was rescued The Driver, and my sister had to come up with another plan. When I realized this, I had to join them to be a part of it, figure out what they had planned before they initiated it. Then you killed The Driver. But at the last minute, he said something to you that crushed you. He knew your weakness. How did he know that? Think. Who had the training to come up with that profile, to understand you and your motivations, weaknesses? Who could have told him how to reach your Achilles' heel and make the most of it?"

Nick was confused. He'd realized The Driver knew his weaknesses before. He'd assumed The Director had provided The Driver with information on him, what motivated him, understood what made him tick, and how to exploit it. It was infuriating.

Finally, he said, "Who?"

"I had no idea how this had happened at first. I made a few very gentile inquiries and learned there had been a woman you took from the missile facility, a forensic psychologist. It finally made sense. She'd been conspiring against you and Bexx for her own survival. You let her in the back door and never even realized it. She fed The Driver information on you for her own benefit, trying to form alliances and survive. My guess is, she also fed my sister information on how to manipulate Bexx. You wanted her dead, Bexx stayed your hand there, but Bexx was equally a threat to her survival. She played you both, giving The Driver the tools to defeat you, and Special K the tools to drive you and Bexx apart. My sister wanted Bexx back at any cost. My life included. Making sense now? Bexx ultimately killed her, but the seeds had been planted, the damage done, and you had no idea."

Nick said quietly, "Forensic proctologist. She was a forensic proctologist." He smiled uneasily, stunned at the realization of what Svetlana was saying. How had he missed it? It made sense.

"Well, your forensic proctologist was moving pieces around on the chessboard like a champ, and no one even had a clue. She did it right under your nose. Do you see why I had to play their game to know what they were doing? Your focus was on The Director, my focus was on them. Someone had to watch your back. My life depended on your success as much as your own. My sister is lethal, and she had her sights set on winning Bexx at any cost."

Nick nodded. Her story made sense, but it didn't explain everything.

"So, you were on the inside, waiting for the right moment to tell me what was really going on. Working your sister, earning her trust when she had no idea you knew it was her who suggested to The Director that you be kidnapped and brought here, to lure me out into the open. That's what you were doing?"

"Yes, that's correct."

"Then why leave when the team left? You could have stayed and broken ranks. You were never Asgarda anyway."

"Something happened I didn't see coming. Bexx left after she saw your meeting with The Director. She sat on the roof of the facility and wouldn't allow anyone else to come up. Apparently, she watched through some kind of video feed and finally came down and told the team we were all leaving. I had to press her hard to find out what had happened. She finally admitted you had won, you had defeated The Director."

"Tell me, what was it that was unexpected? What happened?"

"She told Special K she made a deal with someone who wanted to hire the team. They would even the odds for you in exchange for hiring the team and Bexx as their leader. She said at the last minute the security around The Director was called off and told to stand down. Then you made your move and killed him. Her condition for agreeing to the new benefactor was that you never be included in the team again. She felt your influence was too disruptive. Too toxic."

"She told all of this to your sister, and in turn, she confided in you?" Nick asked. "How do you know Special K wasn't lying, feeding you bad information like she'd done before?"

"When Bexx tasked me to kill you, I knew. My sister had no idea that was coming, I could see it on her face. Total surprise and elation. At last, you'd be removed from the equation, and Bexx would be her's."

# CHAPTER TWENTY-SIX

It was a lot to process. Nick sat motionless, putting the pieces together in his head, playing back the TAC team response to the order to stand down. He knew then something was up, someone wanted The Director dead as much as he did. If Bexx was behind it, why didn't she tell him in the note she'd left under the C-4? She knew he'd survived, he realized that now; she would never have left the note otherwise. How the hell could she have known? It never occurred to him. She knew because she'd been watching. They had no other communication. There was no reason for her to leave the note if he'd died. Jesus! And now she wanted him dead!

"Damn!" Nick whispered. He felt sick.

"So?" Nick pointed at her left hand. "Why the broken finger? Why did Bexx kick your ass and then send you on a mission to kill me?"

Svetlana smiled, and a small giggle escaped from her chest.

"What?" Nick asked, puzzled.

"Yes, that...well, it didn't go down like she'd hoped?"

"What do you mean?" Nick pressed further.

"She suggested we have an argument, a physical fight even in front of the team. I agreed. It would serve her purposes and mine. As I said, I'm guessing she wanted to know if there were any team members who had second thoughts about the new direction they were headed. Fighting me would draw them out. And if there were none, it would enable me to make a clean break from the team and complete a mission with no assistance. Prove my worth to them as an Asgarda. As you said, I wasn't one of them, (and here Svetlana carefully added), and I'm still not. She wanted to choreograph the dispute, plan it. I said no. I wanted it to be organic and unplanned. Like you, I prefer winging it and letting the cards fall where they may. So that's what I did."

"And? What happened?" Nick asked, curious.

"When she least expected it, I confronted her about leaving you. Abandoning you after all the team had survived because of you. And now following a new benefactor. No loyalty at all. Not even a backward glance. I insulted her over and over, telling the truth as I saw it. Not the carefully crafted story she wanted told. She was furious and challenged me to a fight. So, we fought."

"And she kicked your ass, and then you came here under her direction - and she believes you're still loyal?"

Nick knew otherwise. The letter still in his jacket pocket described her mission more or less, leaving out the minor detail Bexx had sent her. Caught between two women again, which was the least lethal? If Nick had to guess, both were equally lethal, but was either really on his side? That was the real question that needed to be answered.

Svetlana smiled. "I held my own against her. That, she didn't see coming. I guarantee that."

"What do you mean?"

"It was a draw. We fought for just over half an hour. I broke her nose, ripped out handfuls of her beautiful black hair. Your beautiful Bexx isn't so beautiful today. I can promise you that."

Svetlana's eyes burned with a simmering anger, and Nick saw she meant what she said. It was hard to imagine. He'd fought Bexx as well, and she'd bested him. She was formidable. Perhaps he'd underestimated Svetlana. Then he remembered JT had been training her! Of course! That was it. JT had street fighting skills and professional training as well. Anyone trained by him would benefit from that combination.

Nick sat back in his chair and looked at Svetlana. Her face was battered, finger broken. But her spirit was intact. She didn't look like a woman who had been defeated by Bexx in battle.

"Another beer?" Nick asked.

Their burgers were gone, fries too. Funny, he didn't remember eating the fries, but they were gone, and the longneck bottles of Bud Light Lime were both empty.

"Yes, please," Svetlana replied.

Nick got up and walked to the ordering area of the small café and asked for two more beers.

The cook reluctantly retrieved them. She'd overheard bits and pieces of their conversation. The facial expressions and eye contact between her odd daily lunch customer and the new beaten and battered woman made her very anxious. They were both obviously very intense people. She just wanted to close the café and start the day over tomorrow but saying that out loud now to either of them seemed unwise at the moment.

Nick returned to the table and placed both beers on the table. "You finished?" he asked and nodded to the plates on the table.

"Yes."

Nick picked up the plates and returned them to the cook, making sure to remove all the silverware from the table, especially the knives. At the counter, he palmed one of the knives and slid it up the left sleeve of his jacket.

Svetlana smiled; she was in. He was listening, more importantly, hearing what she said and what it meant. He would never have bought her another beer and cleaned up after her if he had not heard and in some small way believed what she had said. The cleaning up after the meal was something she had seen him do many times in the missile facility. He had done it for Bexx then, instinctively. Now he'd just done it for her. Predictable; he couldn't help who he was.

Nick returned to the table and handed her the beer in his right hand, keeping the beer in his left arm at chest level. He sat down and said nothing. The silence continued as he waited. Her story was over, the line of shit she had prepared had been delivered. Now she was flying with no flight plan. Where to go from here, she hadn't planned, that was obvious. Nick's eyes watched everything as he waited. The silence grew ominous. The tension in the room was now obvious.

Svetlana sensed something had changed; what, she didn't know. Perhaps she had misread him? She felt increasingly uncomfortable as he sat and stared at her. Had she missed something? What was he waiting for? She decided to wait and see what happened. She wished she would have kept the plate and silverware from the meal now. She had no weapons, and Nick was watching as only Nick could.

Five-minutes of silence passed, and the cook couldn't take it anymore. "Hey, you two, I need to make a run to my house. Would you mind taking this outside while I close up?"

Nick didn't move. "How much to leave the café open? I'll lock the door when we're finished. Just flip the sign when you leave, saying you're closed. My friend and I have some things to work out."

The cook stuttered and stammered, "Uh, well, I would prefer..."

"Two hundred for the use of the café for the rest of the day. I promise I'll lock up when we're done with our conversation," Nick said, his eyes never leaving Svetlana.

"Sir, I, um, I don't think that's appropriate," the cook replied.

"Three hundred," Nick replied.

The cook relented. "Three hundred cash?"

Nick removed his wallet and handed it to her. "Take whatever you need. Flip the sign to closed on your way out."

The cook took money from the wallet and handed it back to Nick. She looked at his face; he never broke eye contact with the woman at the table but reached for the wallet when she handed it back over. The cook left in a hurry, turning the sign to "Sorry we are Closed." The café was now theirs; they were alone.

Finally, Nick spoke. "So you kicked Bexx's ass and took the mission. So far, so good. I follow you. It sounds like you're still on Team Bexx and came to ghost my ass. Or did I miss something?"

Svetlana stared right back at Nick. "No, you didn't miss much at all except the part where I was protecting you."

"Protecting me? Protecting me from what? The Director is gone, dead, looking like a very real victim of the Tooth Fairy. Do you know who the Tooth Fairy is, Svetlana?"

"I'm guessing you aren't referring to the childhood version of the story, so I'd say no," Svetlana replied.

"No, I'm referring to a fellow traveler, fictional, but a brother in arms. Never saw the movie *Red Dragon,* I'd guess?"

"No. I haven't," Svetlana replied again.

"Sorry, I digress. How exactly are you protecting me again?" Nick spoke quietly.

"I..." Svetlana swallowed and stammered. "I came to warn you. I told you what's happened and why just like before when you put the keylogger on my computer. I'm being honest with you. What do you want me to say?"

"Why are you here?" Nick spoke menacingly; the rage barely contained under his voice. "You didn't come without an end game. A plan. Now you're here and confessed all. It all makes sense, I agree. Everything except what you've left out."

"And what's that? What have I left out? I told you everything," Svetlana said, confused.

"Now what? That's what you left out. Now what? Do you follow me back to the facility and we fuck like rabbits? Do you confess your secret love for me and we fall madly in love and hide from the world behind three-foot thick walls of concrete? Now what?" Nick was ramping up."-Do I turn my back on you three months from now and you complete the mission, killing me and gaining a foothold in the Asgarda? Or perhaps after you kill me, you and your sister simply take the facility and leave Bexx and her Asgarda to their own devices. Answer my question. Now what?"

"Now? I don't know," Svetlana replied. "I guess I hoped we would solve these next steps together. You and I working together. You beat The Director, and I've been watching your back with the team. Now you have all the pieces. I guess I could leave if you like. The choice is yours, Nick. We can work together, or you can go on alone and hope the next time Bexx sends someone to kill you, you see it coming."

Nick stared at her for several more moments. He slid the knife from his sleeve and dropped it on the table. Then he reached inside his pocket and retrieved the letter. Svetlana felt her heart skip a beat, then another. Perhaps he'd shoot her right here. Watching him reaching in his jacket, she began to wonder if she'd made the wrong play. Misjudging Nick would be fatal.

Nick pulled out the letter and threw it across the table. "Read that," he said

Svetlana pulled the short letter from the envelope and opened it. Reading it, she smiled.

"See, I told you I kicked her ass. She's really pissed now!" Svetlana smiled as she looked up at Nick. "Now she wants us both dead and hopes we'll do it for her. She'll clean up what's left."

"Still doesn't answer my question. Why should I trust you? I've survived this long without your help, and let's be honest, the whole idea of Bexx flipping a switch and going from protecting me and being pissed off at the risks I take to wanting me dead is a stretch. Very thin indeed. What proof do you have besides your word?"

Svetlana didn't flinch and reached inside her own pocket. Nick lunged across the table. "Easy, girlfriend. Been there, done that." The knife that had been on the table was now pressed at her throat so fast, she barely saw him move.

She nodded and continued to remove a small tape recorder. "I have it all on tape. Every word your protective Bexx said." Svetlana put the microcassette recorder on the table and pressed play.

# CHAPTER TWENTY-SEVEN

Svetlana sat back and watched as the story she'd told Nick unfolded now in Bexx's voice. The reaction she observed was nothing she expected. At first Nick stared at the recorder, eyes unblinking, absorbing the conversation. When he heard Bexx say, "Does it matter? We're a team of mercenaries. We've been hired to do a job. If the identity of the target changes your feelings about the mission, then perhaps you shouldn't volunteer," Svetlana saw a tremor start in his left hand. Moments later, he erupted. Svetlana had heard stories about the gas station in Mosby Montana, and even more unbelievable, Nick's assault on the water tower at the facility. Now it suddenly all seemed very possible.

Nick stood, his entire body shaking, fists clenched, sounds coming out of his mouth, unintelligible words. His entire body tensed, back arched, legs locked. A roar escaped from Nick that sounded inhuman. Svetlana felt her breathing increase, and she realized she felt terror. Looking at Nick, she realized he no longer saw her, no longer saw the room they were in. Whatever this was, it was at Nick's core, something he could barely contain, and now it was loose. Svetlana quickly shut off the tape recorder.

Nick grabbed the table they'd been sitting at, which had been permanently affixed to the floor with four large bolts. He ripped the table out of the floor and smashed it repeatedly against anything nearby. Over and over, he brought the table down against the ancient wooden floor and surrounding tables until it finally came apart and flew in pieces around the room. Tables adjacent to them were smashed, chairs in pieces.

Finally, Nick stopped, and breathing heavily he took a deep breath and screamed, "You lying, deceitful fucking bitch!"

Svetlana looked at the damage in the diner and thought *the cook probably should have held out for more money.* Nick left the café and climbed into the F150. The truck roared to life, louder than Svetlana had remembered; it was as if the truck had been betrayed as well. The motor's RPMs much too high, Nick dropped the transmission into reverse, and the tires began to spin immediately, rocks spraying under the truck and against the outside wall of the café. The truck pulled out of the dirt parking lot and spun around. Nick dropped it into drive and was gone. Svetlana stood, stunned by the eruption. She wrote a quick note on a napkin that said they'd had an accident and would make full reimbursement for the damages. She left it on the counter and then got into her own truck. Backing out of the parking lot with much more care, she headed towards the missile facility. Hopefully, that was where Nick was headed as well.

While Svetlana drove, she ran through possible scenarios in her head of what would happen when she arrived at the facility. None of them ended well. She was committed, however. There was no turning back now. Svetlana finally arrived at the facility and found Nick had left the gate open. His truck was outside, door closed, and the motor turned off. She took that as a good sign; he was at least operating on autopilot. Following patterns and habits well entrenched in his mind. Svetlana pulled up to the facility slowly and stopped her truck. Shutting off the motor, she listened for a moment. There was nothing, not a sound, just the constant wind cutting across the North Dakota landscape, daring something to rise up in its path. She got out of her truck, grabbed her small bag of clothes and toiletries and began to walk cautiously towards the facility. Svetlana found Nick sitting in the kitchen area of the facility, staring at his now broken and bleeding hands. Two fingers were obviously broken, and the fingernails of all the fingers of his left hand had been torn off in the violence at the café. Nick looked at his hands curiously, as if he wondered what had happened. Svetlana put her bag down and went to retrieve a small first aid kit. She returned and cautiously approached Nick.

"May I look at your wounds now?" she said quietly, taking another step towards Nick.

Nick didn't respond. Finally, she was close enough to sit down and pulled up a chair in front of him. Slowly, she reached out and took his left hand into hers and began to clean the wounds. Nick didn't flinch as she pulled off one of the last fingernails that stubbornly hung on to the finger it had called home. It didn't come off easily; the last few bits of flesh refused to let go.

Finally, when he was cleaned up, she said, "Would you like to lay down?"

Nick didn't respond. His body trembled from the remaining unspent adrenaline still coursing through his system. Svetlana helped him up and walked him to the room that had been his and Bexx's. She sat him on the bed and then slowly lowered him to the pillow and covered him with a blanket. Seeing Nick this way, broken, was eerie. It was surreal to realize the same man she'd been so afraid would kill her a few moments earlier was now shattered. Svetlana thought about the letter Bexx had written to Nick, announcing her arrival and preparing him to see her as an assassin. She had no idea what the recording of her conversation had done to Nick. If she wanted him dead, this would have been the easiest way. Just lie, betray him. He had no defense against that. It was painfully obvious Nick had some deep dark secrets that tormented him. They had risen today when he least expected it, and she hoped he'd be able to recover. They had work to do.

It took several days for Nick to recover mentally to the point where he could carry on a conversation. Svetlana brought him meals, and occasionally he would take a bite of a sandwich or piece of fruit. It was slow going. Finally, one day he got up, swung his feet over the side of the bed and got up. He undressed and took a shower, shaved several days' growth off his face and got dressed. He removed the bandages from his hands; fingernails needed air to heal. He'd learned that the hard way after the water tower incident.

Walking up the stairs to the kitchen, Nick opened the metal door.

Svetlana stood at the kitchen counter, preparing some fruit and yogurt in a bowl. She wore a cut off tee shirt and nothing else. Nick stared at her, nearly naked, making her own breakfast.

She looked up and smiled. "Hungry?" she asked playfully.

Nick walked into the kitchen, pretending to ignore the fact that she was mostly nude. "I am, but not for yogurt and fruit."

He opened the freezer and pulled out a bag of *Foster Farms* precooked chicken patties. Taking out two patties, he put them on a small plate and then put the plate in the microwave.

Svetlana began to eat her breakfast and pretended not to be aware of Nick staring at her.

"I'm guessing you sleep in the nude," Nick finally spoke.

"Yes, sorry. I'm a bit of an exhibitionist. Hope you don't mind."

"Mind? Why would I mind? Doubt you'll be here long. Feel free, walk around nude all you want. Hell, spread your legs on the table. I don't give a shit. Means nothing to me. Probably picked up a few cool tricks from your former employer; show me what you learned at the Meat Market, Svet. Go ahead, impress me with your marketing skills."

Svetlana scowled at him. "Don't be a dick."

"It's kind of my thing, Svetlana. Haven't you heard? So, if you don't want me to be a dick, get dressed. Not that you don't have a world class ass. You do, it's perfect. It's just I don't need the frustration. Respect my boundaries, and I'll try to respect yours."

"Okay," Svetlana replied, and putting down the spoon and bowl of yogurt, she turned and walked towards the door. She didn't have to turn to see if Nick watched her walk away.

Nick watched as the door closed behind Svetlana. "Jesus," he whispered. "I don't remember her looking like that in Vegas."

JT's workouts had transformed her. She was cut now and moved more like a well-muscled cat than a tweaked-out stripper. Nick thought back to the van when the girls had stripped her of all clothing and jewelry, removing even the body piercings to keep The Director off their trail. He hadn't remembered her being so fit then. Three months of Asgarda training hadn't hurt either. She'd nearly bested Bexx in a fight. A few more moments and Svetlana returned wearing a pair of skin-tight leggings and a workout shirt.

"Better?" she asked, spinning around in a circle on the floor, smiling as she twirled. "Aren't I cute?"

Nick raised his eyebrows and finally just shook his head. "Ya, sure, I guess. So, what's the plan here? I mean, you were sent to kill me, so Bexx will be expecting some kind of feedback sooner or later."

Svetlana replied, "I don't know. I have no plan. I plan on taking it day by day. And since you mentioned Bexx, isn't she also going to be expecting a reply from you? She did warn you that I was coming. What do you plan to do about that?"

She had a point. Nick shrugged. "Okay, day by day. What's your plan today?"

"Gardening, weeding, and watering," Svetlana replied and walked outside.

What? Gardening? Had he heard her right? Nick got up and walked to the door, opened it and looked out. Svetlana had been busy while he sorted out Bexx's betrayal. There near the facility was a twelve foot by ten-foot patch of earth that apparently she'd dug up with a shovel. In it were rows of what appeared to be vegetables planted and marked with seed packets.

How long had he sat in his room? Then he realized, Shit! The *Versa-Climber!* The C-4! The whole facility was wired to blow if he didn't hit the Versa for twenty-minutes every other day. Why hadn't it gone off?

He realized the answer was kneeling in the dirt, pulling weeds twenty feet away.

"You found the Versa?"

"Oh, yes. Your phone alarm went off. You'd finally fallen asleep, so I checked it. The only alarm on the phone said, '*VersaClimber* twenty-minutes'. I figured it mattered enough for you to set an alarm. So, I did a twenty-minute workout and checked the machine. Nice boobytrapping there, Nick. Expecting company?" Svetlana smiled a playful smile and brushed the hair back out of her eyes. "Come on, help me pull some weeds."

Nick knelt in the dirt and started pulling weeds. "Did you disable it?"

"No, I just set the same alarm on my phone. I figured if you felt you needed the insurance, it should probably stay in place. Besides, I like the workout. It's very intense and makes me all sweaty."

Nick said nothing, but secretly he was impressed. No one had liked the *VersaClimber*. It was much too hard for the rest of the team, but he reminded himself Svetlana wasn't Asgarda.

# CHAPTER TWENTY-EIGHT

D ay by day turned into a week, then another. One day, Svetlana found Nick outside the facility, staring off into the fields in surrounding area. He was anxious, pacing, and his hands came out of his pockets and then went right back in. She watched him and wondered how much longer. They both knew they were waiting for the other to make a move and hoping it would never happen. As things were now, this wasn't sustainable. Eventually, something would break, and the house of cards they'd been living in and pretending was stable would not only come crashing down, it would explode.

"What's up?" Svetlana said as she walked up to Nick, who was pacing.

"I need to go to the post office, and I don't know why. I don't want to know if there are any letters there. I don't want to know if Bexx has sent anymore. I don't care. But it was part of the routine that got me through the day, and then the week. And…"

"And? And what?"

"The café. If I remember things correctly, and I'm not sure I do, it feels so weird when I think back. Like I was riding on the shoulders of a monster, watching the show through a dirty window. It's hard to recall, but at the very least I need to apologize and replace the things I damaged."

Svetlana smiled and picked up a dried piece of grass from the wild grasses that grew in the area, put it in her mouth, and twirled the tip of it with her tongue. She smiled a playful, seductive smile as Nick watched her.

Finally, when she felt she had his full attention, she said, "Already took care of the café. When you were working through Bexx's betrayal, I went into town and paid them twice the cost of replacing what had been damaged."

"How did you explain what happened? They didn't call the cops or in this case the sheriff's department."

Svetlana shrugged. "Simple, I told them what they wanted to hear. I told them you'd had a seizure and blacked out. They believed what they wanted to believe. If I told them you ripped the table out of the floor and smashed up the place in a fit of rage they'd never let us come back. That'd be stupid. Dresden is a small town. And besides, I like their burgers. So, when we do go back, they'll be very sympathetic and welcome you back. And they'll have new tables and chairs." Nick nodded and quietly said, "Thanks."

"So, if you need to go to the post office, let's go. I'd guess there won't be a single letter. She'll wait for one of us to contact her. Whoever survives will reach out to her, that's what she expects. She had no expectation we're speaking honestly to each other. That's not in her tool chest. Honesty. At least not this kind of honesty. And since we're being honest, let's be clear: I know you're waiting to see what I do next, and vice versa. We both wonder how long will this truce hold."

Nick nodded and met her intense gaze. This kind of honesty was addictive. It was a drug that made the very real threat she posed seem worth the risk.

Svetlana continued. "Besides, I need to go to the post office as well. I have a package coming, and I need to ask the postmaster about some shipping options. So, let's go. Remember the last time we went there together? We had fun. It doesn't have to be a Bexx moment; it can be a Nick and Svet moment."

Nick agreed. The need to return to the routine he'd used to navigate the day was intense at the moment, and his anxiety was barely containable.

When they reached the post office, Nick got out and checked the post office box; there was nothing. The box was empty as usual. Then he asked the clerk, "Anything for me in general delivery?"

A quick check revealed no letters, no packages. Nick nodded and felt the tension melt away from his shoulders, and a smile erupted on his face. The clerk stepped back, alarmed. Nick had been coming daily for months, and never, not once, had he smiled. Now seeing him smile, it felt out of character, alarming even.

Svetlana saw the change in the clerk and stepped in to diffuse the situation. Speaking to Nick, she smiled and said, "Would you go next door and order for us? I'd like what we had the last time we were here, minus the seizure of course. Let's hope that doesn't happen again any-time soon."

Nick nodded, puzzled by the clerk's reaction to him.

Once Nick entered the café, his surprise was doubled. The cook greeted him with concern. "How're you feeling? Better, I hope. That must have been a doozy of a seizure! Feeling better?"

Nick smiled uneasily. "Yes, better, much, thanks. Sorry about the, uh, damage."

"Oh, no worries. Your friend explained everything and more than reimbursed us for the damage." The cook smiled. "Really, it's fine. What will it be, then, the usual?"

"Yes, the usual. Make it two. My, uh, friend will be here in a min-ute."

"Excellent, two bacon burgers with fries coming up. Here's the long-neck Bud Light Limes."

Nick nodded and returned to the place where he'd sat before. A new table and chairs were there, this time not mounted to the floor. Nick sat and waited for Svetlana to finish at the post office.

In the post office, Svetlana asked about shipping options for per-ishable items. The clerk suggested FedEx or UPS for anything perish-able. The post office had no way to keep perishable items from spoiling should they arrive late or if she was unable to come immediately and pick them up.

"Good to know. Thank you," Svetlana replied and left the building.

Once inside the café, Svetlana sat down and picked up her beer. Raising it towards Nick, she said, "cheers!" and they clinked bottles.

"What was that about?" Nick nodded towards the post office.

"Worried?" Svetlana smiled.
"Always cautious, yes. Worried? No," Nick replied.

"That's a surprise," Svetlana replied. "Someone has a birthday coming, and I wanted to prepare for it."

Nick was confused. Birthday? It wasn't his birthday. "Whose birthday is it?" he asked.

"Mine, silly. You should know that. My sister said you've read everything there is to know about me. You should've remembered that."

Nick nodded. "Sorry, birthday wasn't a fact that helped me find you. It was a part of the entire picture. I needed to know your age, to understand what potential kidnappers would have understood made you an asset. A commodity."

Svetlana nodded and continued. "I wanted to order some perishable items for a dinner I have planned. Would you celebrate my birthday with me?"

Nick nodded. "Sure. I mean, of course." Nick felt uncomfortable and squirmed in his chair. "Uh, what does the target of your next ordered kill buy you for a birthday gift?"

"A nice bottle of wine would be perfect. Something that would go well with lamb."

Nick's eyebrows raised. "Wine? Really? Red okay? Any preference?"

"Red is fine. I like reds. You pick. I trust your taste in wine."

"In wine?" Nick said, smiling. "Meaning?"

"Well, let's just say wine is something you can't really screw up. Relationships seem to be a challenge for you. Your taste in women, that needs some work."

Nick nodded; "touché." He raised his bottle again, and again they clinked bottles. The burgers arrived a few moments later, and they ate.

When they were done, Nick asked, "How long do I have to order the wine?"

"Two days. I'll order the lamb when we get back to the facility."

"Okay, thanks." They left the diner after the cook waved goodbye and said, "Please come back." Nick nodded uncomfortably and mumbled, "I liked it better when she didn't speak to me."

Svetlana already knew he would never be able to secure the wine in time for the dinner. He'd have to make a trip to Grand Forks. She'd checked, and the nearby wine and liquor stores had a very small selection of red wines. They were in beer country. Decent reds would be hard to come by. That would give her time to make her real plans. She had to get to the roof and check the VSAT and be able to do it with no interference. If Nick caught her on the VSAT, her plans would be in shambles and what little trust she had built with him would evaporate. She couldn't afford that now.

Nick searched and came to the decision Svetlana expected. He went on to explain that he would need to leave for Grand Forks immediately to pick up the wine. He finally found her in her garden.

"Hey, the nearest place I can get the wine is in Grand Forks, so if you really want a red with the lamb, I'll need to go get it now. Is that okay with you?"

Svetlana nodded and stopped her gardening for a moment. "Sure, that would be great. Do you mind if I stay here and tend to the garden?"

"No, no problem. I'll grab the keys and head out. See you tonight?"

"Sure, drive safe," Svetlana said and smiled. Just for a moment, Nick saw something. Just a glimpse of something else behind the smile.

"Yep, safe," Nick replied.

Nick pulled out of the facility and drove for about five-minutes and then turned around. He'd left his wallet intentionally to enable him to have an excuse to return. If Svetlana was up to something, five-minutes should be enough for her to feel comfortable enough to drop her guard.

Nick drove slowly back to the facility and coasted in the last five hundred meters. The engine idled as he pulled in the missile facility driveway nearly silent. Svetlana was still in her garden and hadn't heard him pull in.

"Jesus," Nick whispered, "what's wrong with you?" Nick chided himself, thinking, It's her birthday, not yours. Not like she's planning to ambush you by inviting you to her birthday dinner.

Nick got out and slammed the door. Svetlana looked up, surprised.

"Sorry, forgot my wallet. Glad I realized before I was all the way to Grand Forks."

Svetlana smiled. "No doubt. Good luck." She turned back to the garden.

Nick felt like an ass lying to her, but he'd seen something hidden in the look she gave him as she suggested he go alone to get the wine.

# CHAPTER TWENTY-NINE

S vetlana listened as the truck pulled back out of the driveway. That had been close, too close. She checked the GPS tracker app she'd installed on Nick's phone and saw he'd pulled out and again was leaving the area. She'd just made it to the garden when his truck came back in sight of the facility. So far her plan was working, but that had been uncomfortably close. Thank god for GPS.

When Svetlana was sure Nick was genuinely on his way to Grand Forks, she climbed to the missile facility rooftop and accessed the military VSAT. Turning it on, she read the last few messages between Bexx and the new benefactor. Bexx was serious about removing Nick from the team, that much was clear. She wanted him out. Special K was working her magic on Bexx that far back, influencing her to leave Nick. No worries.

Svetlana typed on the keyboard, *Are you there?* and pushed send.

A few moments later, *Yes, I'm here* came the reply, and then *Who is this?*

*I was sent by Bexx to conduct a mission here at the missile facility in North Dakota. I am to relay through you that the target will be acquired in the next forty-eight hours. I recommend plans be made to return here within the next fifty hours to complete the mission. Will you relay?*

*Affirmative. What is your current mission?*

Svetlana nearly typed in, *Elimination of Nick Hudson* but then stopped. Why was the benefactor asking what the mission was? The benefactor was the one who ordered the mission, at least according to Bexx. Svetlana sat back and thought for a moment. She shook her head slowly; Bexx had lied to her. The benefactor had no idea what her mission was and apparently had not ordered Nick killed. She was stunned. She had to think quickly. Finally, she decided no response was the best response and shut down the VSAT terminal.

"You bitch!" Svetlana said menacingly.

Bexx had no intention of letting either of them live. If Nick had killed her, Bexx would have returned and finished him. Now it was clear that if she killed Nick, Bexx would return and finish her.

Svetlana sat for a minute on the rooftop. Finally, she thought, no matter, I'll press on with my plan. Two can play this game.

Just over two hours later, Nick arrived in Grand Forks and decided to pick up a case of red wine. No point in making the trip for a single bottle when you could buy a case. He stopped in *Happy Harry's Bottle Shop* and grabbed a cardboard box to fill up with red wines. Twenty-minutes later, he was checking out. Happy Harry's had a fantastic selection of wines, and Nick specifically picked a bottle of *Stone and Bones,* a blend from Portugal for the lamb dinner Svetlana had planned.

Nick was back in the truck and on his way to Dresden after filling up the truck at a local *Loaf n Jug* gas station.

Nick arrived back at the facility four and a half hours after he'd left for the wine. He had no idea Svetlana had sent her message and had her own epiphany about Bexx's plans for the two of them. She didn't destroy the café after her epiphany; instead, she'd widened the path and scope of destruction far past what she'd previously planned.

The next day, the lamb arrived via UPS and Svetlana began preparations for her birthday dinner. When it was nearly finished, she called Nick to the kitchen and asked him to go get ready for dinner.

"There was a gift for me from you on your bed. Would you mind putting it on?" she said matter of factly.

Nick was puzzled. "What? A gift from me to her on his bed?"

He turned and walked to his room. There on the bed was a charcoal striped suit, dress shirt, tie and matching shoes and socks. On the dresser were a set of matching cufflinks and tie tack.

Nick raised an eyebrow. "Okay," he whispered. "Guess I need to shower and change."

Nick returned to the kitchen and found Svetlana had changed as well. She wore a charcoal black midi dress, form-fitting with clean lines. Her shoes made a clipping sound as she navigated the kitchen Nick saw she was wearing dress shoes, black high heels, with straps that crisscrossed her ankles. He noticed she wore no nylons as well.

Nick took a deep breath. "So, dinner? Is it ready?"

"Nearly. Would you pour the wine?"

Nick recovered the *Stones and Bones* from the fridge, and Svetlana looked at him questioningly. "Chilling a red? Really?"

"Really! You'd be amazed what a little cold does to the experience of a red. What was normally a complex experience in a red wine is now tenfold as it warms up. You'll see, trust me on this," Nick said confidently.

"Really? I can't wait," Svetlana replied. "Dinner is nearly ready. Have a seat."

Nick watched as Svetlana brought their plates to the table. "Perhaps you'll let me cook for you next time. I mean, if there is a next time," he said.

Svetlana smiled. "Of course. That would be great."

She picked up her glass and held it up towards Nick. "A toast?"

Nick picked up his glass. "Happy Birthday!"

Svetlana laughed. "That's not a toast!" she said and clinked her glass against his.

They laughed and talked while they ate. Nick was surprised at the lamb she'd prepared. It was excellent. Svetlana did have to admit; maybe Nick had something with the chilled red. It was much more complex as it warmed and mixed with the dinner's seasoning.

Finally, they finished, and Svetlana stared at Nick silently, refusing to break eye contact. Uncomfortably, he said, "More wine?" and got up before she could answer. Returning to the table, he began to speak.

"Really, thank you for the meal, and the suit. Not the usual exchange for a birthday gift; historically, I give a gift on the other person's birthday."

Svetlana nodded. "Understood. You'll give me a gift later, trust me," she said confidently.

"And if I refuse?" Nick said, understanding immediately what she meant.

"You won't."

Nick was slightly offended. "Oh, really? I won't, or I won't be able to refuse?" His tone was suddenly angry. "Listen, I appreciate…"

"I know you appreciate the dinner. I heard you," Svetlana cut him off. Suddenly angry herself, she put her wine glass down.

Nick continued. "Look, you don't have to give me the full court press. Let's don't make this something it isn't. You were sent here to kill me. I'm supposed to kill you. This has been a nice dinner. I've really enjoyed your company, but the real world is out there. Our world."

Svetlana looked confused. "Full court press? What does that mean?"

Nick continued. "It's a basketball analogy. A full court press is usually in the last two-minutes of a game. Normally when a team scores, they run to the opposite side of the court and wait for the offense to attack. In a full court press, they challenge the offense immediately. They get up in their faces, hands up, looking to steal the ball or disrupt the opposing team's play in any way possible."

Svetlana smiled and took a drink from her glass. "Sounds physical, sweaty, intense. And who knows where your hands might end up."

Nick, clueless, said, "It is! It can be exhausting, especially coming at the end of the game. It really tests your conditioning and concentration."

"I see," said Svetlana, "and it's only for two-minutes? What a shame!"

Nick nodded, realizing now she understood exactly what he'd meant by the reference and had baited him. He'd fallen for it, hook, line and sinker. Svetlana stood up and took his hand. Moving closer, she slid his hand up under her dress.

"Care to demonstrate the full court press, Nick?"

He stood up and attempted to move away. Too late. She pulled his hand between her legs, and he was done. Nick let out a low moan.

"Yes," Svetlana said seductively. "Tell me again all about the how the hands disrupt the play?" She put down her glass and took his. "Give me your other hand," she demanded.

Nick woke up later that night and looked over; damn, it had been real. Svetlana was asleep facing him, curled up in the blankets with only her face exposed.

Nick thought, *how cliché, the ex-cop and the ex-hooker, each hell-bent on killing the other, end up having amazing angry sex.* Nick took a deep breath. Well, she hadn't killed him, and he had to admit she could have at any time. He was completely vulnerable. Then another thought, *Damn, Svetlana was good.*

Nick smiled. Bexx had been a very different lover. Svetlana was more his equal. Angry, damaged, demanding and uninhibited. He hadn't been shocked by her. She seemed to understand when to move and how, intuitively, when to speak and what to say. She had a filthy mouth and had been very unpredictable. Bexx had been the exact opposite. She had a script she followed; much like the rest of her life, she planned and prepared everything. Svetlana just rolled with it. Nick had to admit, they were much more compatible, mentally and physically. They both played off the other's needs.

Nick closed his eyes and thought, *Easy man, don't get played by a player. She's been a hooker, a high end one at that. Don't be manipulated by sex. That's all this is for her, sex. Could be with you, could be with the farmer across the county. She doesn't care. Neither should you. Wake up!*

Nick turned to look at her again. *Damn, she's beautiful. So what if she was a hooker?* All his caution melted away. *Screw it, day by day!*

He rolled over and woke her up, his hands sliding under the blanket and exploring her now familiar muscular curves again.

# CHAPTER THIRTY

The next morning, Nick rose early and walked to the kitchen and made his habitual breakfast: two Foster Farms chicken patties nuked in the microwave. When the microwave finished heating the patties, the alarm bell went off, and Nick removed them and placed them on the counter. As he opened the drawer to retrieve a fork, the door opened and in walked Svetlana, still sporting bed head and wearing nothing.

Nick smiled. "Morning."

Svetlana made a small hand wave back and stumbled to the fridge. She leaned down to grab the carton of orange juice while Nick watched.

He took a deep breath and let it out, thinking, *Damn, I could get used to this. No stress, no Director, and...no clothes.* Nick smiled and began to cut up the chicken patties.

"So, what's the plan today?" he asked.

"Don't know, just got up. I'm still trying to understand that basketball analogy from last night, the full court press?" Svetlana asked mockingly. "Interesting strategy." She raised her eyebrows and asked in a sarcastic tone, "Any other basketball analogies you'd like to share?"

"Well, there is the three-point shot," Nick fired back immediately, "but that takes a lot of practice."

Svetlana laughed. "Practice, huh?"

She finished the glass of juice and walked to the door. "I'm gonna shower and then go check the garden. Maybe later we could talk?"

Talk. Nick had heard that before. "Talk" was woman code for don't get too comfortable, don't think for a minute this will last. Talk was code in Nick's world for Danger, Will Robinson, shields up! Mr. Scott won't be able to save your ass today. The Warp core is about to go nuclear. The

Klingons have made a truce with the Borg and Captain Kirk has jumped sides. Stick a fork in this; it's over.

Nick swallowed hard and nodded. His appetite was suddenly gone. He pushed the plate away and stared at the door that had just closed.

"Jesus, woman, get it over with. Why draw me in, just to nuke it and watch me burn?" he mumbled. "Screw this shit!"

Nick got up and went to the F150 and got in. Starting the motor, he backed the truck out of the garage and drove off.

Svetlana finished her shower and walked to the kitchen. Nick was gone, breakfast unfinished. Something she said had struck a nerve, a big nerve. He'd left, and if he didn't come back in time, the day would go to shit and fast. Bexx was on her way with the team. They were a few hours away, how close exactly she didn't know. Time to check.

Svetlana checked the GPS app and saw Nick was now at least fifteen miles away, driving random back roads, turning this way and that. "Something's on his mind, that's obvious." The driving pattern had no pattern. He was just moving to move.

Svetlana pulled up another program she'd found on The Driver's computer. It enabled remote access to cell phones. It wasn't the standard program available on the Web; it was government, black ops software. Cutting edge and very effective. Svetlana turned on Bexx's phone just in time to hear her briefing the team on today's mission.

"Our new benefactor has secured a position for us in their operations. Today, we'll retake the missile facility. I've sent Svetlana ahead to subdue Nick as a test of her abilities and willingness to join our team. Svetlana has sent word that she's been successful. When we arrive at the facility, we'll verify Nick's status and then secure the facility. Once the facility has been secured, we'll proceed to the second part of today's mission. Unfortunately, our benefactor has discovered Svetlana is working against us and has been from the start. Special K will brief you on the remaining details. When she's explained what the benefactor has learned, I think you'll all agree Svetlana and Nick both need to be removed from the equation before we can continue as a unit."

Svetlana was stunned as she listened to her sister detail events and conversations that had never happened. It was all fiction; all made to make their mission more palatable. When Special K completed the mission brief, the entire team was in agreement: Nick and Svetlana would have to be killed when they arrived at the facility. Svetlana turned off the app. She checked the GPS; Nick was farther away now. She needed him to return, so she texted him.

*Must have struck a nerve, please come back so we can clear the air?*

Svetlana pushed send on the text and waited.

*OMW*, was all he sent back.

OMW? She tried to work out the meaning. Oh my word? No, that couldn't be it. She Googled it. OMW was standard text for On my way.

Svetlana began to set up her plan in earnest. T minus three hours and counting until Bexx arrived. An hour later, Svetlana heard the truck's motor in the distance. Nick was back and cutting it close. She took a deep breath and muttered to herself, "Sorry for this, but there was no other way." Then as he pulled up, she said, "Game face, remember game face."

Svetlana smiled and sat on the concrete ledge Nick, and Bexx had sat on months earlier while they discussed their plans to defeat The Director. She'd retrieved two Bud Light Limes from the kitchen fridge and waited for Nick to approach her and then offered him one.

Nick was different, guarded now. Gruffly, he sat down. "So talk," he blurted out.

"What's wrong?" Svetlana said.

"Nothing. Get on with it, spill it! Last night was blah blah blah, but that's never gonna happen again. Got it. Big mistake, blah blah, too much wine, which is bullshit! Why draw me in like that, just to blow it all up? I'll never get what women get out of being demolitions experts.

Like, what's the plan now, Svet?"

Svetlana was quiet. Nick was hurt. That much was obvious.

She took a drink from the beer and asked a question. "Did you love Bexx?"

"What? What? Did I love Bexx?" Nick looked at her, puzzled. "Did I love Bexx? No, I don't believe in love. Love is a myth; love is bullshit. Show me someone who tells another person they love them, and I'll show you someone who's about to be screwed over royally. Love? You can't be serious? No, I didn't love Bexx. Do you think she loved me? Based on her actions now, I would guess yes. In the standard definition of love in my world, she loves me very much, and that's why she wants to kill me. Shove that shit down someone's throat, and you can cut their nuts off, and they'll thank you for it. To hell with that." Nick took an angry draw from the longneck bottle and swallowed twice. "Next question!"

Svetlana looked at the cement below their feet, then took a drink from her bottle. "I don't believe in love either," she said. "I believe in today. Here, now. Here and now is all that matters. I try not to plan anything. I nearly finished school in Germany. That was the first time I believed a plan would actually pan out. Then my sister used me to draw you out. I didn't see that coming."

She looked at Nick. "I like you, Nick, simple as that, but I don't plan. So all I had to say when I wanted to talk was to ask can you do that? Live for today? If this goes south, no harm, we just part ways. By being honest with ourselves and each other even when it might be painful, I think this could be healthy, you and I."

Nick was stunned. "Seriously?" He expected the usual "I'm so attracted to you, but…" speech. "But" was the keyword, it meant -Everything I said previous to "but" is bullshit, and here's the truth: I'm gone and have been for a while now, sorry to deceive you. I could have been honest, but why bother? It's so much more fun to blow this up and watch you squirm.

Nick waited for the "but" exception. Svetlana just looked at him and waited.

"Uh, yes, I mean, I can do day by day. Hell, that's how I've lived for as long as I can remember."

Svetlana smiled and put down her beer. "Can I give you a hug?" She asked.

Nick's eyes narrowed. This was too good to be true, but he couldn't say no. He was programmed to respond to this. He wanted to jump up and refuse. Every previous experience in his entire life told him not to believe her. She was hiding something, planning something, but he didn't care. Nick had a huge blind spot in his drive for survival. Svetlana had discovered it and exploited it brilliantly. Nick put down his beer, and she reached towards him and embraced him.

"Thank you," she whispered, then she drove the needle-syringe she had hidden in the waist of her sweatpants into Nick's right trapezius muscle. Svetlana pushed the plunger down, rapidly emptying the contents into the muscle.

Nick cried out, "Ouch! What the hell was that?"

Svetlana threw the syringe and said, "What? What's wrong?"

Nick pushed her away and rubbed the right side of his neck; it stung. He looked at her and said, "Something stung me. Felt like a bee or something stung my neck. Are you okay? Did it get you?"

Svetlana said nothing and watched as the drug took its effect. Nick stumbled, his vision blurred. He looked at her and tried to say, You bitch!, but "You" was all that came out before he blacked out and dropped to the ground.

Svetlana checked his pulse, rolled him over and checked his pupils. "Sorry, Nick, the team is coming to kill us both. They're an hour or so away, and I needed to make damn sure The Wild Card wasn't in play. I make the rules in this game. Wish me luck."

# CHAPTER THIRTY-ONE

S vetlana ran back to the facility to Nick's room and grabbed a set of his handcuffs. Then she hit the garage and picked up a roll of duct tape just to be sure. After watching him rip the table out of the floor in the café, she wanted to take no chances on his escape when he the drug wore off. To say he would be angry was an understatement. He would be furious. Trying to contain a freshly erupting volcano might be easier; better not to let it erupt at all.

She returned and found Nick exactly as she left him. She kicked his foot just to be sure he wasn't trying to draw her in by playing possum. He wasn't; he was out cold. Svetlana pulled Nick's arms in front of his waist and handcuffed them. Then she dragged him across the field to the very same silo where he'd dispatched The Driver and opened the hatch access. Dragging him down the stairs was much easier than crossing the field. Gravity helped, and she was grateful for the assist. Time was rapidly slipping away. She had much to do before Bexx arrived, or it was all over. When she finally had Nick at the bottom of the thirty-five-foot depth of the silo, she took out the duct tape. Taking a page from JT's playbook, she wound the tape backward several times around his legs and then tore it off. Next, she wound a couple of rotations around the sticky tape with the tape facing down, making the tape appear to have normally been placed. She repeated the process around his handcuffed wrists, and finally, she bound the wrists to the feet. She kept at it until the roll of tape was completely spent.

Svetlana surveyed her work and hoped it would be enough. She didn't cover his mouth; if all went as planned, she would need his fury to be real. She had to sell the idea to Bexx he'd in fact been subdued - as if there were any doubt about that - but she had to sell it completely. Her life depended on it. Last, she searched his pockets and retrieved his cell phone. She opened the clock app and set the timer to fifteen-minutes. This was a gamble; she assumed she would have at least fifteen-minutes before Bexx would order her death. Svetlana ran the metal stairs, skipping every other one, up the thirty-five-foot stairway and reached to top barely winded. She opened the door and sprinted across the field to the facility.

Inside, Svetlana went straight to the armory and retrieved one of the Romanian AK-47 pistols and all the AK-47 magazines. A small insurance policy, but now details mattered. She took the pistol and the magazines to her truck and placed them behind the seat. Then she pulled the truck out of the garage and parked it in front of the entryway door approximately twenty-five feet from the door. All set, and not a moment to spare. A Black Chevy Tahoe drove through the now open facility gate without hesitation. The Tahoe stopped, and a man got out. His face bandaged lightly now, he looked like he'd been severely burned recently. Most of the injuries had healed, but his face was severely disfigured.

"I think you're lost. You may want to turn around," Svetlana yelled out.

"I know where I am. Is she here yet?" was the disfigured man's reply.

"Is who here?" Svetlana suddenly had an ache in the pit of her stomach. More variables, more pieces to watch and worry about.

"Bexx and the team. Are they here yet?"

Svetlana smiled. "No, she should be here any minute." She closed the distance between them, smiling, and reached out her hand to his bandaged hand. "I'm Svetlana, and you are?"

"Ian. The Director called me Ian. I was his driver and personal assistant until Nick spit vodka all over him and lit him on fire. Me too, for that matter, but I survived. Do you have him? Do you have The Wild Card finally subdued?"

"I do, but you'll have to wait for Bexx to arrive to verify that fact."

Svetlana tried to reassert some control over the situation before it spun perilously out of her ability to orchestrate. It was critical that the timing of her plan remains viable. Like a conductor leading an orchestra, she needed this symphony to be flawless. Ian's face was disturbing and disfigured. She tried to ignore it.

Ian paused for a moment and assessed Svetlana. He wanted to see Nick dead, personally wanted to put a bullet in his head, letting him know exactly who it was that had finally killed him. However, if this woman had, in fact, subdued him, she too was formidable. Bexx had sent her for a reason. He decided he had enough scars and still healing wounds, no point in needlessly adding more to his already battered body.

"Sounds good. How long do we have to wait? Do you know?"

"Exactly? No. I do know she's due to arrive at any moment."

Ian nodded. "I'll wait in the car, then," he said, then got back in the Tahoe.

In the silo, Nick was starting to regain consciousness. His eyes opened slowly and tried to focus. The floor he was lying on was cold. He tried to look around and get his bearings. What had happened? Slowly, the details came back, and his breathing increased. Svetlana had drugged him, and now he was inside one of the silos, bound with duct tape. He started to get angry and then stopped; he had to conserve his energy. Wait until the opportunity presented itself. He may get only one chance. Nick took deep breaths and finally suppressed the rage, his heart rate returning to something closer to normal. Nick inch wormed his way to the wall of the facility and then sat up.

There in the middle of the floor, he had turned The Driver into something resembling the character *Pinhead* in the movie *Hellraiser. Clive Barker* would have shit himself had he watched the real Pinhead achieve his interesting look. Nick smiled at the thought. Some people wrote horror, others lived it. Above ground, Ian had just arrived, and Nick had no clue. The silo was deep, and ground noise barely registered that deep.

Forty-five-minutes later, Bexx and the team arrived in two Chevy passenger vans. Svetlana's heart raced, but her breathing remained the same. She had to keep her composure. She stood her ground and made Bexx come to her. As she stood in front of the facility, Bexx approached the Black Tahoe, and Ian got out and introduced himself. Bexx introduced the rest of the team. Watching, Svetlana deduced they'd never formally met. The introductions were unnecessary otherwise. That told her much. Bexx had made plans, other plans. Plans no one knew about.

Svetlana whispered to herself, "The bitch has no clue. Excellent." She stared stone-faced as Bexx and the team approached.

"Commander." Svetlana nodded, speaking first.

"Svetlana, do you have Nick subdued?"

"Yes, he's in the number one silo, handcuffed and duct taped. I drugged him and dragged him there. He's waiting for your inspection, and I assume dispatch."

Bexx watched for some hint of deception in Svetlana's manner of speech. There was none.

"Lead the way, please," Bexx said, not as a request, but as a barely veiled command. Her disdain for Svetlana was obvious.

"Of course, Commander." Svetlana held out her hand toward the direction of the silo and said, "Follow me, please." She walked across the tall grass, listening for any sound behind her to indicate an imminent attack. None came.

Once they reached the silo, Svetlana turned and waited for the team and Ian to arrive. She waited for Bexx to open the door.

Bexx wisely said, "Please open the door for our guest." She didn't believe Svetlana had actually subdued Nick and wasn't about to be the first one through the door.

Svetlana opened the doorway hatch, and Ian stepped through first, stopping to allow his eyes to adjust to the darkness. One by one, the team entered and stood at the top of the metal stairway. When their eyes adjusted, they saw there on the floor below, Svetlana had left Nick bound but not gagged. She had, in fact, subdued him and survived.

Ian called out to Nick, "Remember me, you cocksucker?"

"Ian, is that you? The tactical ass wiping specialist. You look like an extra from that *Indiana Jones* movie. You know, the one where they find the Lost Ark. I think that was the title, *Raiders of the Lost Ark*. Remember the German guy in the trench coat? His face melted like butter on a hot griddle. That's what you look like, Ian. How's the sex life now, brother? Women throwing themselves at you now that you look like a movie star?"

What was left of Ian's face was now red with rage. "Laugh it up. I'll put a bullet in your head soon enough, Wild Card."

Nick smirked. "Will you, now? Well, I'd be lying if I said I haven't heard that before. Good luck, foreskin face. It's raining bullets, and I'm still here!"

Bexx stepped forward and spoke. "Nick." She nodded.

"Queen bitch," he returned. "Good to finally see you in all your dyke bitch glory. How's the carpet tasting today? Dusty, I bet. Like licking a well-worn wood floor. Plenty of nasty foot traffic there, I bet. It's been a while for poor Special K. Stuck in her room with no one but a couple of rosy palms and ten fingers to help her get off. I assume you two are back together."

Bexx didn't reply. Special K spit towards Nick but missed. It was a long way down.

Nick turned his attention towards Svetlana. His rage erupted. "Well played, very well played," he said in a low, dark voice. Then he screamed, "Pray I never get free! I will shred you! Understand me? I will rip your lying heart out and eat it while you fade away, you bitch."

Bexx smiled for a moment; perhaps she would give Nick his chance to do just that, after the facility had been secured. She'd like to watch them fight to the death. She hated Svetlana, and Nick released from the duct tape that held him, free to do to Svetlana whatever his twisted imagination could come up with...that would be a sight.

Bexx turned and spoke directly to Svetlana. "Shall we? Let's return to the facility, and you can brief me on the details of your assignment."

"Yes, Commander," Svetlana replied.

# CHAPTER THIRTY-TWO

Nick sat on the cement floor of the silo in complete darkness. The door had closed, and the team had left. He had some time left, time to try to work at the duct tape and try to get free. He may not escape this time, he knew that. Svetlana had reeled him in expertly. However, if he got the chance, he might be able to drag a few unlucky bastards with him. Ian would be a nice goodbye gift, and if he got the chance, Svetlana too.

Nick shook his head. Damnit, how stupid could he be? Once again brought down by a woman. She was right, he was better at choosing wine. Women were a complete blind spot. There was a reason for the *Samson and Delilah* story of the bible. Few people realized the concept was repeated over and over in ancient text. Jael defeats Sisera, and Judith beheads Holofernes. Some scholars claim the significant difference in the accounts of the three women defeating powerful warriors of their times is that Delilah sold out to her people's enemies, making her even more treacherous. Nick couldn't have cared less about their motivations. The single most crucial point in his mind was the warriors were defeated by deception, and each had a significant blind spot to their own weaknesses.

"Welcome to the club, dumbass," Nick mumbled to himself as he began to try to stretch the duct tape restraining him.

In the dark, he twisted and turned his ankles and wrists working hard against the silver tape. It was moving much too easily, sliding up and down his lower legs and wrists. Nick was confused. Unable to see what was going on, he had to rely on touch and feel. Finally, he was able to feel the tape that had contact with his wrists. It had been put on sticky side out. Nick stopped. Why would she do that? It made no sense. It didn't work in his favor; it was much easier to stretch the tape when he could use the resistance of the sticky side against his skin. However, it was much more painful. The smooth side against his skin made the tape move when he twisted and flexed. He'd seen this method of binding before in Vegas; JT had bound her like this when she fought back. It made removal of the tape easy and much less harmful to the person being restrained.

Duct tape was very unforgiving to the skin when it finally adhered. It could rip pieces of flesh off when removed. Nick was baffled. Why would she do this? Ultimately, he decided it didn't matter; he needed to quit going down rabbit holes and escape. He had to find a way to fight back. There had to be a way. Then it occurred to him, every other time he'd been bound, he'd also been gagged. Svetlana hadn't gagged him. He could use his teeth. Nick smiled. There was always a way out. He went to work on the tape, biting and tearing as best he could. Spitting out small chunks of tape, he began to work his way towards freedom.

Fifteen-minutes later, he heard gunfire. Not just any gunfire. Nick listened; there was only one sound like that in the entire world. It was the AK-47, singing the only song it knew, its favorite song. Nick listened to the rapid sound of rounds being fired and then a pause.

"Reloading," he said out loud.

Thirty rounds had been fired, they'd need to reload. The sound of the gunfire began again. Sounded like a firefight or slaughter. Nick listened again; only one AK-47 was firing, the gunshots didn't overlap. Nick's eyes pierced the dark, searching, while his ears did the work. He tried to imagine what was going on above. It sounded like a one-man battle. One gun, firing over and over. Then silence. Nothing. Absolutely nothing.

"That can't be good," Nick thought out loud.

He started tearing frantically at the tape. A few moments later, the doorway in the top hatch of the missile silo opened. Nick looked up at the light that exploded into the darkened missile silo. His eyes burned at the blinding brightness of it. Nick squinted and saw the outline of a woman; she held in her hands an AK-47. There was only one reason to bring the AK into the silo.

"Shit! Time's up, game over."

Nick relaxed as he realized this time there would be no escape. The door closed as he listened to footsteps coming down the metal stairway.

Finally, they reached the bottom of the stairwell and the lights inside the silo came on.

~

Svetlana reached the main facility just ahead of the team and opened the door, leading the way onto the main above ground living quarters and kitchen. She began by briefing the team, Bexx specifically.

"As you can see, the facility remains much as it was when we left. I've cleaned up a bit. Nick had left the facility in a bit of a mess." Svetlana walked towards the armory and pointed inside. "Everything is as we left it, Commander."

Bexx looked inside and saw the cache of weapons and ammo. As she did, Svetlana started the timer on Nick's cell phone and placed it in a nearby drawer. Fifteen-minutes and counting; Svetlana had to survive for the next fifteen-minutes. Bexx conducted a mental inventory of the armory. Something was missing, but she couldn't recall what it was.

"Would you like to see the rest of the facility, Commander?" Svetlana asked.

"No," Bexx said, annoyed that she couldn't recall what was missing from the armory. She wanted Svetlana to shut up and stop interrupting her train of thought.

Bexx turned towards Svetlana. "So, tell us, how exactly did you subdue Nick? I fought him once, and it was brutal. We destroyed the farmhouse, and I ended up with a nasty scar on my leg. Special K tried to fight him, and he knocked her teeth out. How is it you defeated him without even a scratch?"

"Not only defeated him but bound him up in duct tape," Svetlana replied. She needed to stretch the conversation out, ten-minutes and counting.

"I watched how Nick beat my sister senseless, and when I was tasked with this mission, I realized going straight at Nick would be pointless. Arouse his anger, and you're fighting an uphill battle. I decided it was best to keep Pandora in the box. Why let Nick be Nick?"

Svetlana let the silence stretch as Bexx waited for her to continue. Bexx was annoyed. Why had Svetlana stopped her explanation?

"So? What did you do?"

"I seduced him. I used Nick against Nick. Every man has a weakness, Commander. And every woman knows it exists. I simply gave Nick a reason to drop his guard. And by the way, he was more than willing to be seduced. He was like a starving child, asking for more," Svetlana said, chiding Bexx. "Apparently, he's been very unhappy sexually for a long time."

Bexx was silent, her face red. Once again, she'd been ridiculed by Svetlana. The implication was clear, Svetlana was better in bed than she was, and Nick had appreciated it. Commented on it.

Bexx recovered quickly. "Of course, not all of us can be a professional sex worker, Svetlana. And some apparently take to the work with an enthusiasm others find offensive."

Svetlana simply replied, "Yes, Commander" as she smiled sweetly.

The team milled around, quietly listening to the back and forth between the two adversaries. They were waiting for Bexx to give the word, and they would subdue Svetlana and put her in the silo with Nick.

"So, you slept with him, how creative. Very warrior-like. Something to be proud of, I suppose, using sex to subdue and destroy a man instead of combat," Bexx continued, her feelings about the strategy Svetlana employed was obvious.

Svetlana nodded. "It seemed more prudent. I felt given Nick's past, he would be more vulnerable to sexual manipulation than combat. Admittedly, he was much more vulnerable than I'd ever hoped possible."

Her implication was again obvious. Bexx was livid. She'd had enough and was about to give the secret command she'd established with the team before their arrival at the facility to subdue Svetlana when an alarm went off in the area around the armory.

"What's that?" Bexx asked suddenly and to no one specifically.

Svetlana answered, "Sounds like an alarm or some kind of timer. Is it your phone, Commander?"

Bexx grabbed the phone in her right jacket pocket and checked. "No, not my phone. Your's?"

Svetlana checked her own phone, playing along with the ruse she'd devised. She needed Bexx to reach the correct conclusion on her own, or at the very least with minimal assistance.

"No, Commander, it isn't my phone!" She looked up at Bexx, alarmed.

Svetlana started to pace. "What could it be? I've never heard that alarm. Not once the entire time I've been here with Nick," she reported, gently nudging Bexx towards her eventual epiphany.

Svetlana waited. The pressure now was on Bexx to answer the riddle. Bexx frowned, she felt manipulated by Svetlana again. Somehow, she'd turned this moment into a challenge of her leadership. Svetlana looked to her for the answer, subordinating to her command when it advanced her agenda. Challenging her when it didn't.

Bexx looked at the armory; the empty shelf bothered her. What had been present before that was missing? Then she caught the faint whiff of the scent of motor oil in the air. Nick had set a booty trap!

"Asgarda, on me, now!" Bexx screamed. "Booty traps! Nick has booty trapped the facility! Get out now!"

Svetlana turned to the door immediately. She had to be out first, and to the truck before the team realized how vulnerable they were. Previously, The Driver had flushed the team out of the facility in a more passive way. He'd stayed inside while they'd faced a sniper in the water tower. Svetlana hadn't been present for that attack. But she'd heard the story and realized it was a flaw in the team's training. They relied on Bexx for direction. They didn't or couldn't think for themselves; when she barked a command, they obeyed. Svetlana just needed her to bark the right command at the right moment. She had.

Svetlana exited the facility ahead of the majority of the team. Bexx stayed behind to make sure everyone made it out and came out last, following Ian and closing the door. She made sure the door slammed, and the team saw she'd remained behind until they were all out safely.

"Everyone here? Everyone safe?" she called out, a subtle reassertion of her command. In the days to come, they would replay this moment in their memories and appreciate her bravery and commitment to the team's safety.

Svetlana continued to the truck while Bexx planted seeds of loyalty in the team. She opened the door and reached under the seat, removing the Romanian AK-47. Grabbing a single magazine, she loaded the weapon and released the bolt. Svetlana closed the door and took the AK off safe and began firing. Thirty rounds later, the team had been cut in half, most crawling on the ground dying. Ian was already dead. Bexx was trying to get back up; a round had shattered her hip, and her right leg wouldn't cooperate with her efforts to stand. No one knew exactly what had happened, it'd all happened too fast. Svetlana dropped the magazine and inserted another, released the bolt and began to fire again, this time more specifically at each team member, making sure they would never get back up.

Finally coming to Bexx, she said, "This was always your weakness, Commander, one-dimensional thinking. You should have listened closer when Nick explained his Star Trek chess. Goodbye, Commander."

Svetlana emptied the clip, shooting the remaining rounds into Bexx's body. Many more rounds than were necessary, but Svetlana had to admit it was satisfying to silence the mouthy bitch once and for all.

# CHAPTER THIRTY-THREE

Svetlana stepped over the bodies after counting to make sure everyone had exited the facility and been killed in the ambush. When she was positive everyone had been accounted for and killed, she returned to the inside of the facility. She retrieved Nick's cell phone and turned off the timer. She then disabled the C-4 explosive charges Nick had placed throughout the facility. She'd set them as a backup plan just in case she failed. If she'd been subdued by Bexx and the team, and maybe killed, she had every intention of defeating them by setting the charges to go off in three hours. Three hours seemed like a reasonable period of time for the team to have settled in and lowered their guard. One way or the other, the team would have been finished today.

Svetlana grabbed a Bud Light Lime from the fridge and walked back out of the facility and over the dead bodies to the silo. Nick was the final piece of the day's tasks that needed to be completed. She opened the door to her truck and removed the spent magazine from the AK. Grabbing another, she inserted the fresh clip into the well and rocked it back into place, hearing the familiar click as the magazine release catch locked it into the well. She then turned and walked to the silo.

Nick stared up at what for a moment looked like Bexx, but then his vision cleared and he could see it was Svetlana. She had a beer in one hand, and the Romanian AK-47 slung over her shoulder, a thirty-round clip in the magazine well. More likely than not, she'd come to finish him off.

*Damn, I am one sick, twisted individual,* Nick thought as he watched her walk. She was incredibly sexy holding the assault pistol in one hand and a beer in the other. The confidence she portrayed, the way she moved. He didn't want to die, but if this was the last thing he saw, Svetlana walking around the silo's concrete floor, pacing like a muscled predatory cat in the zoo...blind spot, Nick reminded himself, they'd all been killed by using their weakness and blind spot used against them. "Screw it" Nick whispered, "at least I'm in good company. Samson, Sisera, Holofernes, and now me."

Svetlana heard him whispering and sat down cross-legged on the floor just out of reach. She drank deeply from the bottle, and Nick watched as her throat contracted and swallowed the beer. Her throat, even there she was delicate and beautiful, and yet lethal. The bottle emptied, Svetlana put the bottle down and let out a loud belch, then laughed.

"Sorry," she said, "that was louder than I'd thought it would be!"

Nick smiled. "No problem."

Svetlana smiled back and sat in silence for several minutes, watching him, assessing him. She saw he'd been tearing at the duct tape with his teeth, a piece was stuck to his lip. Small pieces scattered around him, spread out on the floor. He never gave up. Not once. He had no idea how to quit.

Nick spoke first. "Sounded like the AK-47 singing its favorite song outside. I heard two clips fired, one emptied and then a pause, reloading, I assume, and then more firing." The statement was finished as a question.

Svetlana nodded. "I had to be sure I killed every single one of them. They were going to kill me regardless of what happened here."

Nick nodded. "And you know that for sure, do you?"

"Yes, with absolute certainty."

"How?"

"A black ops app The Driver had in his tool chest. Enables remote activation of a cellular phone. I recorded the conversation, so you could hear it if I survived."

Svetlana took out the microcassette player and pushed play. Nick could hear Bexx's voice explaining to the team they would be dispatching Svetlana when they arrived and made sure he'd been in fact subdued by her. When she completed playing back the recording, Svetlana turned off the recorder.

Both of them were silent for a while as the matter of fact tone of Bexx ordering both their deaths sunk in. She'd displayed more emotion ordering fast food on the trip back from Vegas. It was disconcerting to hear her like this.

Reality hit, and Nick darkly whispered, "Bitch!"

Svetlana nodded. "Sorry I had to take the chance and subdue you. I couldn't risk your unpredictable behavior. I needed you to be genuinely angry at me and them."

"I still am," Nick replied.

Svetlana nodded.

"So, they're all dead? Ian too?" Nick asked.

Svetlana nodded.

"Even your sister?"

"Yes. She had no problem with Bexx's order, and as I told you before, she helped facilitate my abduction in Germany."

Nick nodded. "That's quite a body count for one day, Svetlana. You okay?"

Svetlana nodded. "Sure, it was them or me. If they succeeded in killing or subduing me, I'd already reset the timer for the C-4 in the facility. They would have died anyway. It was an all or nothing play."

"All in, huh? Every chip on the table, including me. Would have been nice if you at least included me in the decision."

Svetlana rolled her eyes. "Nick, you've been throwing yourself at death the entire time I've known you. You take risk after risk. Hell, you went to face The Director with no plan and no backup. I at least had a plan and backup plan if I failed. So, you're tied up on the floor of a missile silo! So what! Quit whining!"

Nick thought it over. She was right. Still, he didn't like it. She'd taken risks with his life that might not have panned out.

"So now what?"

"Now I wait for you to calm down. When you're calm enough, I cut the tape and remove the handcuffs, hoping maybe you'll help me clean up. There is a hell of a mess up there that needs to be cleaned up."

"So, cut the tape, let's go!" Nick said. Svetlana walked to the opposite side of the silo and pulled a knife out from behind some of the electrical conduit. "I put this here just in case they put me down here with you. Always another layer to the plan, right?"

Nick nodded, smiling, stunned at the way things had suddenly turned around. He thought he was dead an hour ago; he just wanted to take a few of them with him. Now Svetlana had succeeded in outmaneuvering them all. She cut the tape and pointed out what Nick had noticed.

"See, I put it on backward. I had no intention of letting you die if I could help it. But I did need the full force and fury of your temper to convince Bexx I'd succeeded."

"Let's be honest, you did succeed. I bought it," Nick said.

"Yes, you did," Svetlana smiled, "and when I realized what that meant, how you felt, it was even harder to press on. I had even more to lose."

She let Nick get up and handed him the key to the handcuffs. "See you upstairs." She turned and walked up the metal stairway while he unlocked the cuffs. Nick followed a short time later.

They both stood in front of the bodies that had been the Asgarda. Nick let out a low whistle. "Damn, I knew you meant it, that you'd killed them, killed them all, but actually seeing it...wow."

Svetlana thought for a moment, "Weird, when Bexx finally reached the conclusion I was hoping for: that the whole facility was set to blow up, she screamed out, 'Booty traps!' And she called the Asgarda to her."

Nick burst out in laughter. "Seriously?"

"Yes, how weird is that?"
Nick turned and looked at her. "It's awesome. You're my Hannah!" he said, laughing.

"Hannah?" Svetlana replied. "What?"

"A television show, *Dexter*. It's about a serial killer who kills serial killers. He meets Hannah. She's a serial killer, and he plots to kill her. At the last moment, he has her on the table, strapped down, and he's ready to kill her. She looks at him with this look..." Nick paused.

"Yes? And?"

He swallowed hard. "She looks at him and stares straight into his eyes with this look that says everything. Verbally, she says go ahead, kill me, but in her eyes you see it. This carnal, fearless, powerful look. She's nude and strapped to the killing table. He holds the knife, and she knows, he's powerless. His threat is empty, the serial killer who hunts serial killers has found his match. He can't kill her. He sets her free, and they have wild, angry, serial killer sex. There was never any doubt in her eyes. She just waited for him to realize it. It's the single most intense moment I've ever seen in any movie or television show, and no one gets it. No one comments on it. I've waited for my entire life to see that look."

Svetlana looked at him, smiling. "Come on, *Dexter*, help me clean up the mess I've made."

After the bodies were loaded into his truck, Nick picked up a shovel and said, "I've got this. I need to do the labor. I have a lot of anger to work out. I was prepared to die a few hours ago, and now I'm burying my enemies. No one left to double cross me. It's over."

Svetlana smiled. "Enjoy the work, then, and come back in when you're done. I think we need to work through that three-point play analogy you mentioned earlier." She bumped him with her shoulder and smiled. "Hurry up! I'm curious."

When Nick returned, he washed the dirt off his hands and stared at the floor of the kitchen area of the facility. Svetlana watched him and asked, "What's wrong? Burying Bexx hit you harder than you thought it would?"

Nick looked up, startled for a moment. "NO! That's not it. She wanted me dead, good riddance. Just another betrayal in a long line of betrayals. I did notice, however, that she appeared to have been shot several more times than the rest of the team. Someone apparently had some anger issues of her own to work out. Huh?"

Svetlana shrugged. "Maybe a little more than usual, yes. Betrayal isn't something I handle well either. She set me up to die, multiple times. And if she hadn't, my sister had."

Nick nodded. "While I was out there, I realized this isn't sustainable. I have no money, no retirement. Nothing. It all died when I died in Panama. Or at least when my identity died. We won't be able to survive here much longer. The truck is stolen. The only thing I own is this missile facility, and it's just a freak set of circumstances that make it mine. Property taxes will be coming up soon, and I can't pay them. There's no work around here, no businesses. Hell, the café depends on us to come in for lunch a couple of times a week just to survive. We won't even be able to do that much longer." The reality of their survival was starting to set in. Nick realized their happy ending was a few hours old and already over.

Svetlana nodded. "About that."

"Yes, I know it's bleak. Sorry to rain on the parade. Reality is, now we have to look forward. The fight is over, but life goes on. Now what? Shit! I never, ever thought I would make it this far. I never cared about the money. We had The Driver and his hacked credit cards, or at least that's what I thought. Now I realize he was on the NSA payroll. He had his own money."

Svetlana got up. "I have something to tell you. Remember when you came to rescue me and Bexx let it be known she was wealthy? My sister told me about it. She said it made her more determined to win her back and force a wedge between you two."

Nick nodded. He remembered she said she was worth something like four hundred million in American dollars.

Svetlana paused. "I'm sorry. I stole it from her. All of it. I was so mad she had betrayed me, I wanted to make sure if I didn't survive her plan, she wouldn't have that money to fall back on. So, I moved it around, broke it up into smaller accounts and then pulled it all back together again in two accounts; one account in the Cayman Islands, and the other in a numbered Swiss bank account. Money won't be an issue. Ever."

"Seriously?"

"Yes." Svetlana was embarrassed.

Nick laughed. "You're embarrassed you stole her money, but killing her doesn't bother you?"

Svetlana's face was red. "Yes! And no, it didn't bother me at all."

# EPILOGUE

Two weeks had passed since Nick buried the Asgarda and Ian. Svetlana had continued her gardening, and they still made occasional trips to the café for a bacon burger. Every night, Nick stared off into the distance. There was something left unsaid between them, and he was trying to figure out a way to say it. Eventually, one night it came to him. He took a deep breath and realized what he needed to say and how.

Nick planned a dinner for the two of them and bought her a new dress. He wore the suit she'd purchased and told her he had a surprise for her. Dinner was on him, and there was a dress he wanted her to wear. As usual, panties were optional; Svetlana smiled at that remark.

That night, he served the dinner, seafood pasta, with *Purple Owl* Pinot Noir. When they were done eating, Svetlana asked, "So what's the special occasion?" She had some idea but didn't want to ask specifically. Nick nodded and told her he'd been thinking about something for weeks and had been afraid to talk to her about it.

Svetlana was uncomfortable. Was he seriously going to ask her to marry him? She made it clear she lived day by day. She didn't want to say no, but she didn't want to say yes either. She waited, nervous.

Nick finally pulled out a set of handcuffs. "How do you feel about handcuffs?" he asked.

Svetlana laughed out loud. "You like the kinky stuff, is that it? Of course, I do. Handcuffs are fine!"

She stood up and turned around and put her hands behind her back. Nick placed the cuffs on her wrists and then double locked them. He turned her around and sat her back in the chair she was sitting in. Quickly, he grabbed a roll of duct tape and a blanket he'd hidden in a cabinet in the kitchen and restrained her to the chair with several quick turns around the chair. Svetlana was a little bit alarmed but still laughing.

"What are you doing?" She stopped laughing when Nick brought out the syringe from inside the inner pocket of his suit jacket.

"I've never done well with betrayal, and I'd guess neither have you given the reaction you had to Bexx's plans to kill us both. You do realize you still betrayed me. You put a needle in my neck and pumped me full of narcotics. Then you tied me up and risked my life to defeat Bexx. The whole thing could have gone sideways, Svetlana, do you realize that?" Nick said, his eyes hard and cold.

Svetlana was in a full-blown panic now; Nick was deadly serious. He was still angry. She had misjudged him, and now she was completely vulnerable.

"Please don't do this. I'm sorry I did what I had to do for both of us to survive. We made it, Nick. We're together, we can live here for the rest of our lives. We fit, sexually, intellectually, emotionally. We get each other's damage. Please don't do this!"

Nick's face was stone. He took the cap off the syringe and pushed the needle in her left shoulder. Pushing the plunger down, he emptied the syringe into her arm. When he was done, he coldly, methodically replaced the cap and placed the syringe on the table.

Svetlana shook her head; No, this couldn't be happening.

Nick continued. "Do you feel betrayed now? I did. When you stuck that needle in my neck, I was furious. I felt more than betrayed. I realized I wanted the life I thought we could have, and then you used that against me to earn my trust and manipulated me. Do you remember? I do. In the past, I've never come back from that kind of betrayal. An act like that would have been a death sentence for our relationship and possibly for you personally. Do you grasp that now?"

Svetlana listened but had nothing to say. She'd misjudged Nick's emotional and psychological damage immensely. Now it would cost her life.

Svetlana just looked at Nick and said "I'm sorry I hurt you. I was wrong. I was desperate. But you're right, I broke you and used your trust in me against you. I'm sorry I can't take it back."

Nick just stared at her. "Too late now, but if you could go back, what would you say? What would you change? Would you want to stay, permanently? Would you use words like love? 'Nick, I love you?'" he said mockingly. "Would you spit that bullshit at me, try to manipulate me even more?"

Svetlana shook her head no. "I thought about what you said about love. I agree, my sister said she loved me and tried to kill me or worse. I think she meant it. She loves me, it meant nothing to her, she never gave a second thought to my death or torture as a sex slave. She didn't really care. I realized you knew this long before I even thought to question it. Love is a myth. People kill each other every day in the name of love. It's a twisted, broken concept. I don't want it."

"Then what is it you feel for me or felt for me before I tied you up and took your life?"

Svetlana realized he meant it. She would die soon, and now was her time to tell him what she felt even though it wouldn't matter. Her course was set. As was his. She had betrayed him and broken him more deeply than she'd understood.

"I guess I'd say I'm sorry. I wouldn't change it though. It had to happen for us to get here. I don't love you. I do prefer you. I want to be here with you. I chose this over everything else the world has to offer. I'm sorry," she said regretfully.

Nick nodded. "So, you would want this to continue, maybe permanently?"

Svetlana nodded. "I would. This is the safest I've ever felt. I've never connected with anyone like we do...like we did," she corrected herself. "I'm sorry I broke that before it ever had a chance to really grow."

Nick nodded. "Are you feeling the effects of the drugs yet? Feeling woozy, having trouble concentrating?"

"No," Svetlana said, puzzled. Nick had dropped in moments. She was still clearheaded.

"So, this is what you think, not some drug-induced bullshit. The drugs haven't hit yet. This is how you really feel?" Nick asked sarcastically. "You wish we could have continued in this life indefinitely." He rolled his eyes.

"Yes, I had hoped so."

"Why didn't you say so?"

"I was afraid you wouldn't feel the same way, and you'd push me away. I felt like if I spoke the words, you'd leave. If I kept it a secret, you'd just live day to day, and we could go on indefinitely," Svetlana admitted.

"Too late now. Say goodbye, Svetlana," Nick said coldly. "You fucked it all up, no coming back to this. You burned it to the ground. Understand? Burned it all to the ground. I see no way forward. It's over."

Svetlana nodded and waited for the effects of the drugs. She closed her eyes and took a deep breath. "I'm sorry."

Nick sat and watched her, waiting. After ten-minutes, she opened her eyes. Nothing had happened; she wasn't getting sick or woozy. Nick just stared at her.

Finally he said. "I needed you to know what I felt. I needed you to understand the despair and hopelessness I felt in the silo. You're right, you needed me to display what I am in those moments. An animal, rabid, furious. Every woman I've ever known has betrayed me, lied to me and used me. Do you understand that?" Nick said.

"Yes, I do," Svetlana said in a whisper.

"I needed you to experience what I felt that day to understand what an effort it was, what it continues to be for me to be here. I put saline in the syringe. You aren't going to die, but you're now going to understand the extreme effort it takes for me to trust you. I'm willing to risk trusting you and dying, rather than going back to day by day. I want more with you, but I needed a way for you to understand the terror I feel. Do you now?"

Svetlana nodded.

Nick cut off the duct tape and removed the blanket, and they both fell to the floor. Nick stood her up and turned her around and unlocked the handcuffs.

He took them off and walked away. As he left the room, he said, "Now, you can leave if you wish. Now you understand how difficult this is for me every day. I choose to stay. I choose to remain vulnerable. I want us to be together."

Nick changed clothes and went outside while Svetlana stood motionless in the kitchen. The ball was in her court now.

As Nick stared at the stars, the door opened behind him, and she came out and stood next to him, handing him a beer.

"You really can be an asshole; do you know that?"

"I do. I've heard it over and over. I couldn't see another way for you to hear me. You needed to feel it, to own it, to understand it. I'm in this if you are."

Svetlana nodded and took a deep drag from the bottle. "We both are. I'm not leaving. But you're still an asshole! You made your point, brutally, I might add. But I do see what you mean. I feel the risk now."

Nick nodded. "A toast, to brutal honesty."

~